MIDLIFE'S A BEAR

MIDLIFE UNLEASHED BOOK 1

RENEE HEWETT

1

JEANIE HUDELSON SURVEYED THE CUSTOMERS HAPPILY painting away in her studio.

The trio of girlfriends at the far table had almost finished their bottle of wine along with their canvases and had spent the last fifteen minutes in a fit of giggles. On the opposite end of the room, one of her regulars put finishing touches on an intricate glass mosaic. The group nearest to the front of her studio consisted of a few mothers with their children. Once they completed their projects, they would need to have their ceramics fired in the kiln.

Every day, Jeanie felt grateful for the life she led. She couldn't believe she'd managed to make such a paradise for herself in Georgetown. Her studio was all she could have ever hoped for: a place where she could paint, but also where she could teach others to love making traditional art.

The studio's closing hours were fast approaching when she noticed trouble at the table with the children.

A few adults huddled around one child, who looked to be on the verge of tears.

Jeanie hurried over, ready to assist. "How's it going over here?"

One of the women looked at her helplessly. "I'm afraid we're just learning a lesson that sometimes art doesn't turn out the way you'd like it to."

Jeanie turned to the child, who had tears filling her eyes. "That's a beautiful mermaid you've painted, though. Can I take a look?"

The little girl nodded, the tears in her eyes belaying both hopelessness and frustrated anger. Jeanie had witnessed it a thousand times. Children had limited patience, but that was okay. Patience could be learned and practiced, and Jeanie made it her mission to ensure they didn't give up on trying.

Not in her shop, no way.

She picked up the little ceramic mermaid and instantly spotted the issue. The figure's eyes were blobs of paint. The little detailed areas always gave novice artists some trouble. Nothing that couldn't be fixed, though. She looked down at the girl. "It's all right. Do you know what's great about art? You can *fix* it! You're never stuck with your first attempt!"

The adults issued grateful thanks as Jeanie took the little girl to the hot air tool, letting her hold it as they dried the paint on the ceramic mermaid. Then, Jeanie painted over the blobs, giving the figurine clean, sparkling blue irises. By the time they finished, the mermaid's eyes were clear, and so were the little girl's.

Jeanie's heart filled with joy to watch the whole group

leave with smiles on their faces. It would be an added bonus when they came back and saw what their projects looked like after being cooked.

When Jeanie arrived home after closing the studio, her husband, Oscar, had already started dinner.

"Hey, hon. How was your day?" Oscar asked. He wore the striped apron that she thought looked so cute on him, and she tousled the back of his black wavy hair before giving him a kiss on the neck.

"My day was good! How was yours?" Jeanie sat on a stool at the kitchen island, and they chatted while Oscar worked on the stir-fry.

After all these years, coming home to Oscar and discussing their days was still her favorite part of each one. He was her husband, best friend, and lover, and their bond had never faded.

She'd had no idea what love could be like before she met him, nor did she have any idea what a fated mate was. She was only a human and hadn't known anything about shifters, but she'd fallen for Oscar, love-at-first-sight-style, and it didn't matter that the man she wanted to be with could transform into a wolf

Now, twenty years later, her and Oscar's love remained just as strong. They'd built a good life together in Georgetown, working on their careers, their relationship, and their home until all were in a place where they couldn't be happier.

As they sat on the back porch eating dinner and watching the sunset over the field, Jeanie couldn't help but think to herself how her forties really were going to be the best time of her life.

Jeanie awoke the following day more lethargic than normal. She'd never been a morning person—always depending on that first cup of coffee to perk her up—but this was different.

I can't be sick, she thought, though she knew it was one of the hazards of working with children. Germs spread through classrooms easily, and sometimes they came into her studio too.

She opened her bleary eyes, wondering what time it was, and found Oscar's side of the bed empty. Since it was a Saturday, that meant he'd already woken and gone for his morning run, which meant she'd slept at least until seven.

She tried closing her eyes, thinking if a bit more sleep would help, but it was no use. Her brain buzzed—awake and active—even though her body felt sluggish and unsettled.

Maybe I just need to get up and drink some water. Maybe eat some breakfast.

She sat up, tossing the covers aside, and a wave of nausea and dizziness hit. She took a moment to steady herself, more determined to leave the bed and find herself hydration and sustenance.

Gotta take care of myself if I want to recover from this quickly.

She swung her legs over the bed, and her feet touched the floor, sinking into the plush carpet, but the moment she attempted to stand, her legs buckled, and she dropped to the ground.

Don't vomit, don't vomit, she told herself as the room whirled around her. She vaguely noticed her cats, Meatball and Chester, staring at her from the doorway with concern on their faces.

She closed her eyes while her stomach churned. *Breathe, just breathe.*

She'd never had a dizzy spell like this, *but there's a first time for everything.* Same with the body aches that grew stronger out of nowhere—she'd almost call it more of a stretching tearing pain than aches at that point.

She kept her eyes shut and focused on her inhales and exhales until the ripping pain stopped, and she finally felt strong enough to try standing again.

She opened her eyes. The room had stopped spinning—a good sign.

She wobbled as she rose, her body feeling unfamiliar and... heavier. *Much heavier.*

When she finally stood back on her feet, she looked toward the two felines in the doorway. Meatball scurried away, and Chester sprang into the air, hissing in her direction before bolting down the hall after his sister.

Well, screw you too, mister. She shrugged it off. If she wanted a nurturing and loyal pet, she would have adopted a dog instead. As it was, she lived with cats, and while they were adorably fluffy and usually silly, they definitely weren't the type to hang around when their owner felt ill.

She shuffled forward to make the bed, eyes mostly still closed, moving on muscle memory since she'd done this nearly every day for twenty years, but when she grabbed for the covers, her hand came up empty.

I guess my depth perception must be off, she reasoned, feeling as though her arms were shorter than normal. *Whatever crazy vertigo I'm having has me all messed up.*

She tried again, making a slow and purposeful reach for the sheets and watching carefully as she did so.

But as she observed her movements, it wasn't her arms or hands she saw stretch out before her. Instead, she gazed at a pair of short, thick, brown, furry arms.

She froze. *What is going on with my mind today?*

She pulled her arms back, turning them, so the palms faced her. She'd never seen anything like it; a huge palm pad, five-toe pads, and some seriously impressive claws at the end of what should have been her fingers.

I must be dreaming, Jeanie thought, closing her eyes and willing herself to wake up. While she did, she touched her face, and there, instead of a nose, she brushed a large snout that ended in a wet tip.

She considered crawling back into bed, but even in her dream state, she didn't want to spread bear fur all over her clean sheets. Oscar never touched them in his wolf form, not in all the years they'd been together, so she reasoned that the dream-bear version of herself shouldn't either.

Not to worry. The loveseat in the living room was her favorite napping spot. She could go rest there until her *real* self decided to wake up.

Jeanie dropped to all-fours and lumbered across her room, passing by her shredded pajamas on her way to the door. There, she realized that her bear backside was a bit too big to allow her through easily, and she had to squish herself through the frame to emerge in the hallway.

Just like Winnie the Pooh stuck in that hole, she thought. *At least I didn't have to ask Meatball and Chester to push my butt through.*

She carefully maneuvered through the hallway, aware that her large lumbering body threatened her carefully hung photos and artwork lining the walls. She did her best not to knock them down and didn't dare look behind her to see how much disarray she'd left behind.

At least she hadn't heard any glass frames shattering.

She'd intended to head straight into the living room for the nap couch, but emerging from the hallway, her stomach rumbled.

Sorry, dream bear, but we're not in any condition to fix ourselves breakfast. She wasn't about to try pulling out a package of oatmeal and a bowl, let alone the kettle for hot water.

Fish outside. The thought popped into her brain as though someone else had said it. She turned to look at the back door and felt *compelled* toward it. Suddenly, she *needed* to escape her house. All thoughts of the nap and waking from the dream were gone. She plodded through the kitchen, bumping into the table and knocking over a chair before grappling with the sliding door's lock and handle. Finally, she could shove it open and poke her nose into the beautiful fresh morning air.

Wiggling herself through the door frame was another issue. *Not sure why my dream brain didn't widen the doorways for me,* she muttered to herself. Once outside, she turned and fumbled with the door again to shut it behind her. Even dream-bear her didn't want the traitor cats to run away—both of whom now sat in the kitchen, staring at her with wide eyes from the other side of the glass door.

She was almost ready to breathe a sigh of relief until she stumbled off the first porch step and tumbled down the rest of them.

No worries, that didn't hurt a bit. Her bear was sturdy—and besides, you didn't actually feel pain in dreams.

She was back on her feet—all-fours, still, as that's what felt right—and headed toward the tree line when a growling stopped her.

She looked back toward the house where a large gray wolf had appeared.

And he looked none too happy to find a strange bear on his property.

2

JEANIE RECOGNIZED OSCAR IN WOLF FORM, HAVING SEEN IT plenty of times in the past twenty years.

"*Oscar!*" Jeanie couldn't speak his name while she was a bear, but she thought it as her bear gave a short roar.

"*Jeanie?*" Oscar's voice came through her mind, loud and clear as though he spoke to her. The gray wolf stopped growling and took a tentative step toward her.

"*Oscar?*" she thought again. "*You're in my dream too?*"

"*Dream? Jeanie, what's going on?*"

"*I'm having a dream that I'm a bear,*" she replied, though she was quickly losing interest in the psychic conversation as the trees once again called out to her. They promised a stream, which would provide her with fish for breakfast. *Yum!*

The wolf ran over to her, blocking her path to the woods before he circled her, sniffing. "*You smell like my Jeanie. And I'd know you, in any shape. You're my mate... but you're a bear. How?*"

For a moment, she forgot about breakfast as Oscar's

scent captured her attention, cocooning her like a comforting blanket. It was so alluring. She couldn't help but circle him once he'd finished turning around her.

When she finished, she stopped at his face. *"This is such a strange dream."*

"This isn't a dream," dream-wolf Oscar said in her mind. *"You're really a bear."*

"Then how am I talking to you?"

"It's the pack link. The same way I can communicate with my other pack members."

Jeanie had learned about the pack link when they were first married, and she'd wondered how the wolves could run together and know what the others were thinking. Oscar had explained that the pack link lets them talk to each other telepathically, but as a non-shifter, Jeanie couldn't access it.

"I guess my mind conjured up this dream to let me know what it would be like to be a proper pack member," she assumed. *"Weird that I'm dreaming of being a bear instead of a wolf, though."*

"You're not *dreaming."* Oscar's tone in the pack link was getting sharper, and she could tell from his wolf's stance that he was losing patience.

Knowing it was useless to debate with a dream person, Jeanie shrugged it off and turned from Oscar, ignoring him as she headed toward the woods.

Then, out of nowhere, an intense pain filled her hindquarters. She roared in protest, spinning around to see that the wolf had nipped her.

She swiped at him, but the wolf sprinted away, too fast to be caught.

"You bit my butt!"

"And you felt it!" Oscar replied via pack link. *"Which means this isn't a dream, right?"*

"I can dream that I felt pain."

"But you actually *felt it."*

There was something to what he said, but Jeanie found it easier to believe in dream pain than that she had *actually turned into a bear!*

"Jeanie, you have to believe it," Oscar pleaded. *"If you don't, you could lumber off into those woods and never come back to me."*

Oscar's voice in her head had turned softer and more worried, a tone she hated since her heart could never let her disregard it. It meant she was doing something that made her husband afraid for her, and if the love of her life was that concerned, she needed to listen. She owed him that much.

She looked down at her paws in the grass. Huge, brown, furry.

And clear as could be. Not that fuzzy, unclear focus that was usually present in dreams.

"How could this be possible?" Jeanie finally asked.

"I don't know, but we'll call Beau and Sandy and find out."

The Mactire pack alpha and matriarch would need to be informed of this new development, and if Jeanie and Oscar were lucky, maybe they'd have some answers.

Oscar shifted back to his human form and tried to coach Jeanie to do the same, but it was no use. Her bear wasn't ready to give back control yet.

Oscar went inside and retrieved his cell phone, returning wearing a pair of gym shorts and chuckling. "The cats are very concerned."

"Not concerned enough to help me in any way," Jeanie informed him through the pack link while she sat in the grass at the bottom of the porch.

"Well, they're cats. What did you expect? It's not every day the person who gives them food and cuddles turns into an apex predator." He laughed again as he poked at his phone, and Jeanie just shook her head.

Typical Oscar, taking everything in stride.

Even his wife turning into a bear didn't rattle him.

"Beau, hey," Oscar spoke into his phone. "I have an issue, and I'm not sure it's one you've ever dealt with before, but my wife, Jeanie, yeah, she turned into a bear."

Oscar turned on speakerphone, so Jeanie could hear Beau's reply. "You two have a fight or something? It's not like you to talk about your wife like that."

Oscar laughed, giving Jeanie a big smile, still trying to offer her comfort even while her distress grew. "No, not that kind of bear. An *actual* bear. She's shifted, and we don't know why."

Jeanie expected Beau to have more questions, but he simply said, "I'm on my way, and I'll bring Sandy too. Jeanie must be upset, and it will be good to have a friend with her."

"Yes, that would be great," Oscar said, hanging up the phone.

It was as though Beau's mention of her being upset pushed her emotions over the edge—or maybe it was just the promise of help being on the way—because suddenly, Jeanie felt wholly overwhelmed and distraught.

This dream feels too real. It's going on too long, and now it's involving Beau and Sandy? What if Oscar's right? What if I've actually turned into a bear?

She braced herself for hyperventilating, but instead, she felt another presence creeping into her consciousness.

Nothing is wrong with being a bear, it said with strong certainty. *This is who we were always meant to be.*

And though the thought was strange, and she wasn't sure she believed the words, her mood stabilized. Her panic dissipated, just *poof*, left her.

In its place, she felt a sort of curiosity as well as pride. Who else went forty years without being a shifter and then suddenly turned into one?

"You okay?" Oscar asked. "You weren't speaking in the pack link, but I can sense your emotions, stronger now than ever before. You went from alarmed to serene in an instant."

Their mating bond had always allowed him to have heightened senses about her, but she'd never understood it before. Now, she did. She could *sense* how Oscar was feeling.

She'd expected worry, but now that she'd stopped trying to go off into the woods, he had none. Instead, she sensed he only felt a calm curiosity, as well as positive assurance that everything was okay, as long as she was by his side.

Oscar was her rock, and he never let a storm set him adrift. Her being a bear hadn't changed that.

"Yeah, it's a lot to wrap my head around, but it's okay. If this is really happening, then it's okay. I'll be okay. We'll be okay."

He nodded. Normally, this would be a time when she'd tuck herself in under his armpit for a hug, but as a bear, she was much too big for that. She wondered if she should try giving him a hug or if that would lead to her clumsily hurting him, but she didn't have a chance to try it because Sandy and Beau's car pulled up.

When they stepped into the backyard, they both assessed the situation.

"How are you holding up, Jeanie?" Beau, the Mactire pack alpha, asked her.

"Holding up okay, thanks," Jeanie replied. *"It's just a whole lot unsettling."*

"A shifter animal emerging later in life isn't unheard of," Sandy added. "But it's rare."

Well, at least there was that. This type of thing had happened to someone before her. Having precedents somehow made the whole thing seem more manageable.

"So, what do we do now?" Jeanie asked.

"Same thing we do with anyone's first shift. We help you to control it so you can return to your human form."

Jeanie grappled with the idea. The serene part of her felt like it was something she could do—shifters go into and out of their animal forms all the time—but there was a tiny part of doubt creeping up, telling her that she wasn't a normal shifter.

What if the bear was asleep for forty years, and now it

was determined to stay out for the next forty in retribution?

She braced herself for the instructions on shifting, but to her surprise, Sandy offered a different suggestion. "Before you try shifting back to your human form, we need to let your bear have some playtime first, okay?"

"*What?*"

"It's what we do with the first-time shifters. Your animal isn't something to be afraid of or ashamed of. It's something to be embraced and celebrated, and it wants nothing more than to go for a run right now. Only once it's had its fun will it be ready to go back inside for a bit."

Her words made sense to Jeanie, especially when she felt a part of her grow happier, the same part that had helped calm her panic earlier—was this part her bear side? She'd always heard shifters talking about their animal side, so she had to assume it was.

Oscar, Beau, and Sandy all stripped and shifted into their wolf forms, and then Beau led them off on a run into the woods.

"*My first pack run!*" she called excitedly into the pack link before she could stop herself. The moment the words were sent out, she realized her mistake. "*I'm sorry, I shouldn't have said that. I'm a bear, not pack.*"

"*Of course, you're pack,*" Beau replied in the link. "*You were pack before you shifted since you were a human married to a pack member, and you're still pack now.*"

"*Even as a bear?*"

"*There are plenty of non-wolf shifters who married into the pack,*" Sandy clarified. "*The only thing that's changed for you is that you now have the added benefits of being a shifting pack member. Like this pack link.*"

"*And pack runs.*" Oscar confirmed her first statement, stopping and turning to face her.

She stopped running, freezing, so Oscar could approach her and then touch his snout to hers.

"*I love you, Jeanie,*" he said.

"*I love you too.*"

And with that, the bear side of her was done with the discussion. It was ready to enjoy the run.

3

———

When they returned from the run, Beau, Sandy, and Oscar helped her tap into the mental link she had with her bear. She promised the bear that it wouldn't have to go back to sleep forever, that she would let it out again.

Happy and satisfied from the run, the bear agreed. Jeanie followed Sandy's instructions to embrace the transformation and return to her human self.

Jeanie was beyond thrilled to see that it worked, so much so, that it almost made her overlook how agonizing the transformation had been.

"It's a little painful at first," Sandy said, offering Jeanie the spare clothes Oscar had fetched for her.

"A little?" Jeanie laughed though every joint in her body screamed that she needed a massage, an Epsom salt bath, and a few days of rest.

"Well, maybe more than a little for those with older bodies," Oscar said, waiting for Jeanie to finish dressing before he wrapped her in a hug. "I'm so glad to see your beautiful face again, love."

They invited Beau and Sandy in for coffee and breakfast, which Oscar mercifully cooked after Jeanie's empty stomach roared—it had been much too long a wait.

While they ate, Beau and Sandy reiterated to Jeanie that she was part of the pack.

"Are you all right with us announcing this at the next pack meeting?" Beau asked. "They'll scent a bear and be curious, and besides, information that affects the pack like this needs to be shared. The sooner, the better."

"I hadn't thought about it, but it's my new reality, I guess," Jeanie said, still fighting the urge to believe it was all a dream. "So the pack—heck, the whole town—will know sooner or later."

Oscar cleared his throat. "Then there's the issue of *how this happened.*"

"We'll definitely be looking into that," Beau assured them.

"We've dealt with plenty of shifters who've been blocked from their animal because of trauma," Sandy explained. "But they've usually known they were a shifter and even had some period of their life when they *were* able to shift. But that's not always the case."

"Trauma-free here," Jeanie said, knowing how lucky she was to be able to say that.

"It's very rare that another shifter *turns* someone else, but I'm guessing that's not the case with you," Beau said. "You haven't had a past encounter with a bear? Bites or cuts or anything."

Jeanie shook her head. "Nope."

"Have you made any enemies lately?" Sandy asked. "Anyone who might want to curse you?"

Again Jeanie shook her head.

Sandy sighed. "That one was the least likely, though. I don't believe I've heard of a witch being able to *give* a shifter ability to someone."

"But they could lock one up," Beau mused, sipping his coffee.

Oscar finished chewing his bite of eggs before asking, "You mean she could have been cursed as a child to have her bear locked up until now?"

Beau and Sandy exchanged a look before Sandy answered, "I think that's a strong possibility."

"Especially since what I sense is that this bear isn't new," Beau said. He looked at Jeanie and explained, "Pack alphas have a stronger sense about some things, and when I first spotted you today, my instinct was that I was finally seeing the real you. That this bear has always been part of you."

Jeanie took a deep breath and tried to digest that information. How could it be that she was supposed to be a shifter her whole life, but only *now* was she able to? She couldn't help but feel as though she'd been robbed. Had someone done this to her? Taken away so much?

The part of her she now recognized as her bear side spoke up.

"The bear doesn't know why it slept this long," she told the others around the table, closing her eyes so she could focus on the message her bear side was sending her. "It doesn't know what woke it. Just all of a sudden, it was here. It feels like there is a lot of life to catch up on. It's missed out on lots of runs."

Sandy placed a hand on Jeanie's arm and gave it a

squeeze. "That's good, Jeanie. Step one was getting you back to human form, and step two is exactly what you're doing—bonding with your animal. Listening to it, understanding it. Just keep doing that for now while we look into all the *whys* and *hows*."

"Thank you," Jeanie said to Sandy. She looked to Beau to add, "Both of you."

"Any time," Beau replied. "That's what pack leaders are here for."

"Are you okay if we go now?" Sandy asked. "Because you're more than welcome to stay with us if you're not comfortable here on your own."

"I feel fine right now," Jeanie said, looking inside herself and not finding any fear or apprehension. "I do wonder about tomorrow, though. If I'll wake up a bear again"—she took a deep breath, forcing herself to admit her biggest point of unease—"and what if this time I have less of my own mind present, and I can't control things at all?"

"That's not going to happen," Oscar said with certainty.

"But how can you know that?" Jeanie asked.

"Because you're my mate, and we're forever linked." He reached out to stroke her cheek, love shining in his green eyes. "I'll always be able to get through to you. That's something I don't doubt for a second."

"Besides," Beau said, standing and heading to the door, "the animals don't take over like that. Not unless it's protecting you from something, which is why it's better to listen to my wife and bond with your bear, so the two of you work together as a team and don't oppose each other's interests."

He held a hand out for Sandy, and they smiled at each other. On their own, they were both exceptional leaders, but together, they were a couple that spread strength, kindness, and warmth to their pack members.

Jeanie knew she was lucky to be in their pack.

Jeanie and Oscar opted to take the rest of Saturday as an easy day. Then, Sunday morning, Jeanie was thrilled to wake up human, though she felt the bear near the surface, itching to emerge.

She ignored it, focusing instead on making work arrangements. She was scheduled to go in and run a mimosas and painting party, but she called one of her other teachers to cover for her. She still needed a day of rest.

A day to wrap her head around what was happening to her.

After the initial shock of becoming a bear, she was starting to recognize the heightened senses she had while in human form. The world *looked* more vibrant and color-ful, all scents were more potent, and she could hear the television on a very low setting.

"It's the bear inside, aware and sharing what it senses with you," Oscar explained.

Thinking about her bear caused the shifting urge to rise again, but she still pushed it away. If she'd told Oscar, he would have certainly taken them for a run, but she didn't want to do it. She was too afraid.

Even though the previous day had ended on a good note, she couldn't grapple with the idea of doing it again —giving up her human body and becoming a bear.

She wanted to reason that the bear was a stranger, and she didn't want a stranger taking over her body, but that wasn't it. When she turned inward toward the bear, she felt endeared toward it—like it was a dear friend who'd shown up after many years away. Even so, she couldn't push aside her human anxiety about letting go and handing the reins over.

We're not handing the reins over. We're just letting the bear out, she tried to reason, but it terrified her to consider it.

It didn't matter if she felt some affinity toward this other existence inside of her. The fact was that the bear had expressed its displeasure at not having been allowed out for years, so what's to say that it wouldn't just decide to rumble off into the woods and never return?

Jeanie couldn't just take Oscar's, Beau's, and Sandy's word for it that the bear wouldn't decide to take over forever. That her consciousness wouldn't fade, and she'd cease to be.

That led her to the frightening thought of what might happen if Oscar went looking for her and her bear refused to listen to him. Would the bear fight her husband? What if she hurt him?

Bear is not a competing force, her animal side told her. *Bear doesn't want to take over.* She started to wonder if the bear side would try to trick her into giving up control.

"What's wrong?" Oscar asked after lunch. "You've not talked about shifting again. I've waited for you to bring it up, but you haven't, though—"

"If you say you *sense* it, I'm going to be annoyed," Jeanie snapped. "I'm getting real sick of that word."

Oscar raised an eyebrow as though to say *too late*. She was already annoyed.

"Yesterday, you talked about being afraid the bear would take over. Is that what's wrong?"

Jeanie glanced at him momentarily before clearing the table and washing the plates.

That was enough for Oscar to know he was on to something. "You have to think about it like anything else, hon. All things in moderation."

"Like alcohol?" she suggested, ready to debate how she didn't need to embrace her bear if it were like an intoxicating substance.

"No, *not* like drinking," he replied, knowing better than to fall for such easy bait. "It's not something external like alcohol is. It's more like your desire to paint. Sometimes you feel inspired and just *need* to run to your easel, right? And you can lose yourself in that painting, going for hours without remembering to eat or drink. But it's not like the *painter* side of you will take over and not *let* you do anything else. You're going to be distracted until you're satisfied, and then you go back to normal."

"My painter side doesn't talk to me like the bear does," she muttered, her back still to him as she dried the dishes.

"Sure, it does. Maybe not as clearly, but it absolutely does. I can't count how many times you've said 'that would make a great painting' over the years. You mean to say that's not the painter side of you speaking up?"

"It's easy for you to lecture me when you've been doing this since you were a kid." Finally, she turned to face him, her arms crossed over her chest, knowing that as much as she didn't want to discuss it, Oscar wasn't about to let the topic go. "None of you—not you, not Beau or Sandy—can *really* know what will happen to me because none of you shifted at forty for the first time."

"You're right. We don't know what it's like to be a first-time shifter at forty." Oscar stood, going to her and placing his hands on her arms. "But here's the thing; we can recognize when a shifter is unstable—when it presents a threat to the human side or to others around them—and yours isn't. Your bear is tranquil, actually. If it wasn't, we wouldn't have been comfortable around you yesterday. I can promise you that much."

Her mind honed in on one specific aspect of Oscar's reassurance. "So it *is* possible for an animal to take over and not let the human back out?"

"Those situations are different." Oscar sighed and pulled her into his arms. "The human has usually suffered trauma. Or there are other extenuating circumstances. You are here, consciously, right now. If you choose to let your bear emerge, your consciousness will stay with it."

She shook her head. She couldn't do it. It was just too weird. She couldn't risk believing Oscar's reassurances. She shifted at forty—no one did that! So no one could predict what her bear may or may not do regarding taking over.

4

———

Returning to work that week, Jeanie was struck by how different everything seemed. The vibrant colors, the extra-strong smell of the paint and varnish, but most of all, the overwhelming and un-ignorable urge to take a nap that hit her on Thursday afternoon when a rainstorm started.

Seeing how she nearly fell asleep while teaching a class, one of the other teachers suggested she take the rest of the day off. Jeanie reluctantly agreed, grabbed her bag, and went home.

The nap couch with her favorite throw blanket looked like heaven when she stepped into the living room, and she fell asleep before her head hit the decorative pillow.

She awoke to Oscar shaking her. "Jeanie."

She slowly opened her eyes, seeing she no longer slept on the couch and realizing she was on the floor. *How had that happened?*

It took her only that second to wonder before the absolute certainty hit her: She was a bear again.

She had no idea why her next thought was to look at the pile of shredded clothes. That pair of pants wasn't cheap, but at least the T-shirt was just a work one. She could replace it with one from the many boxes she had at the studio.

"This is why we have regular pack outings," Oscar lectured. "Shifters make a point to let their animals run, especially during stressful times. Otherwise, it's pent up and gets stronger. If you release it, let it run, then it is less distracting and lets you do your human things undisturbed."

Irritated, she brushed off Oscar's words and focused on forcing herself to shift back into her human form—despite the bear's pleas for playtime.

Only after she was back in her normal skin and heading to the bedroom for new clothes did she realize that all the fears she'd had about shifting had been for seemingly nothing: *she'd had no problems turning back into a human.*

She paused, naked as the day she was born, and looked at Oscar. She didn't have to hear every word he uttered to know what he'd been saying. "Yes. You're right. I had no reason to be so afraid. Yes, I should have been more proactive about practicing shifting this week because it left me vulnerable to the bear demanding out."

Damn bear, tricking me with a rain nap and jumping out when I was unexpecting it, she muttered to herself, though she couldn't really be mad at the bear. She certainly couldn't blame it for doing what it took to get a little time out when Jeanie had refused it so.

Oscar, the wise man that he was, only nodded. *He* wouldn't be tricked into having a fight with Jeanie about her bear. They'd been married far too many years for him to stumble into a fight when she was in an obvious mood.

Jeanie sighed, which ended in a frustrated and defeated growl. "Okay, Oscar. Will you go for a run with me?"

He smiled widely. "I thought you'd never ask."

They left the house—being given cat side-eye from both Meatball and Chester—and then shifted. It astonished Jeanie how easy it was to transform into her bear at will. Just like putting on a winter coat. At least, that's where her thoughts went since when she became a bear, she became much larger and fluffier, which reminded her of how she felt when wearing one of those big puffy coats.

And then they ran.

And it was *fun.*

She couldn't remember the last time running had felt playful and not just like a tedious workout chore. Even the run with the Mactires on Saturday had been more curious, less untethered joy.

When was the last time she *chased* someone, and it had been *fun?*

Sure, she and Oscar might chase each other a bit around the house, but that was usually just a few strides in the hallway. This? This full-on sprint of her bear as she chased her wolf husband was a kind of diversion she couldn't ever remember.

Oscar ran much faster than her. His canine form was built for runs, but her ursine form wasn't, so when he pulled too far ahead of her, he'd make a large loop around, playfully bumping her before he passed her again.

His wolf looked so *happy*.

That was something she'd never seen before. Usually, she only saw him when the entire pack shifted to go for a pack run. Then, his wolf looked stoic. Dignified. Beautiful, but serious.

Now, as he looked back at her, his wolf seemed to be smiling. His eyes certainly shone, captivating Jeanie. How glorious it felt to be liberated in this way with him.

Maybe it's not so bad to be a bear.

Especially with Oscar at my side.

And then she really saw what she'd missed out on these twenty years of marriage. This freedom, *this connection* with Oscar that she couldn't have even imagined before.

For the first time, she felt robbed. Violated. Someone had taken this chance away from her!

Her blood boiled with rage.

Oscar slowed to a halt. *"Jeanie, is everything okay?"*

Jeanie relayed her thoughts to him, and Oscar's wolf response was to approach her and nuzzle her face. *"I understand. I fully expected you'd come around to wanting to figure out who did this to you."*

"I'm not sure finding them will change anything," she replied. *"I think I might just have to go through these emotions as a part of this whole change."*

"I think you're probably right."

Jeanie shook her whole body. *"In any case, I'm not letting whoever might have done this ruin our night. Let's run home. The last one there starts dinner!"*

"We have a special announcement," Sandy called out to the pack at the end of the monthly pack party in their backyard. "A new bear is among us!"

Murmurs went around, and Sandy gave Jeanie a wink.

Sandy and Jeanie had chatted the previous night, so Jeanie would be prepared for being presented to the pack. She hadn't thought it would be a big deal, but now suddenly, she felt nervous. Her bear side knew how important it was to be accepted in the pack, and what if the wolves didn't want her anymore?

"A new *bear*, but this member has already been one of us for many years," Beau corrected, causing even more confused sounds from the crowd. "Jeanie Hudelson!"

Even more shocked noises went through the crowd, and this time, members began turning and looking in Jeanie's direction.

To her relief, they were full of welcoming smiles.

She waved. "Thanks, Beau."

"Now, we know you all have some questions," Beau said to the pack. "We have them ourselves—Jeanie probably more than all of us!—but what we can say here is that Jeanie has been a human member of our pack, mated to Oscar, but now, she's a bear and will be running with us tonight."

The crowd's murmurs were still confused but sounded more approving this time.

Beau and Sandy moved on to other pack business. Once the official meeting was over, they told everyone to eat and have fun. There would be food and chatting for the next hour or so, and then there would be the pack run.

"I knew something was different about you," Claire Shimmerscale, a new-ish member of the pack, was the first to approach Jeanie.

"Really?" Jeanie asked.

"Yeah, you didn't have a shifter scent, but it still wasn't totally human either," Claire replied.

The others around her piped up their corroborating opinions as well.

"I kind of figured it was because you were mated with a shifter, so it was his scent," one added.

"But even so, you still smelled different than the other humans mated to wolves," another said.

They ate and chatted, and Jeanie hadn't felt this much the center of attention since her wedding day. She normally didn't *like* being the center of attention—unless it was for her art classes when she was teaching—but this time, she enjoyed having rapt attention and listening ears because maybe, just *maybe,* one of them might know something that could lead her to figure out how this happened.

Then, the time came to shift and go for the pack run.

It was a regular pack activity that she'd never been part of before. Usually, she stayed behind with the other non-shifters to watch the little ones. They'd go inside, make a big blanket and pillow fort in the den for all the kiddos to snuggle up on while they ate popcorn and watched a movie. The non-shifter adults would have another glass of wine and chat into the night until their mates returned home.

Jeanie would miss it—would miss them. She looked back toward the house, and there were those faces of the other non-shifters peering through the glass. They waved, smiled, and gave her a "thumbs up" signal when they saw her looking.

They were all supportive of her. She made a mental note to make sure she set up a coffee date with them so she didn't lose out on the connection she had made with them over the years.

"You can run with the teens if you'd like," Sandy teased, turning Jeanie's attention back to shifting.

"Oh, don't make her do that!" another woman called.

"Yeah," a third chimed in. "They're all angsty and hormonal. She might be a new bear, but she's still an adult, like us."

"With all the wisdom and maturity that comes with it," Sandy finished.

"I don't know," Jeanie replied with a laugh. "I sure feel like a teen again when it comes to adjusting to a new life change."

"Oh, we're just teasing you," Sandy said. "You're one of us, and you run with us. We'll watch out for you."

"You sure?" Jeanie asked. "Oscar and I have been running, and I'm nowhere near as fast as a wolf. I'm just a lumbering bear. I don't want to hold you back from a good sprint."

"That doesn't matter," Sandy said. "You're *still one of us.*"

That knowledge warmed Jeanie's heart.

"You ready?" Oscar asked, approaching her.

She nodded. Regardless of what her human brain might think, her bear was *more than* ready to go on its first pack run.

She took a deep breath and allowed the bear to come forward, changing her body from human to animal.

Everything was heightened. Her smell, the feel of the slight breeze on her face, and the fact that her animal could see *much* better in the dark.

She hadn't realized that she'd had an audience, but it should have been expected. She turned to face the pack —all mostly shifted or in the process of shifting—and a howl went up—they cheered her!

Then, another howl. This one from the pack alpha, Beau. The rest of the pack joined in with his howl and took off after him toward the woods for their run.

It was perfect, running with *her pack.*

Though she'd never felt left out by not being a shifter, she now had a sense of belonging she'd never had before. She really *was* one of them, even if she was a later-in-life bear.

5

SHE MADE IT THROUGH ANOTHER WEEK OF WORK, MAKING
sure to let her bear out every few evenings. Oscar didn't
mind. He already took regular runs with his wolf, and
now he enjoyed runs with his mate too.

Of course, sometimes he wanted to really sprint, not
lumber around with her, so they did have times when
they separated for a bit, which gave her some alone time
in the woods.

It was good. It gave her time for self-reflection. Now,
she walked the forest, still aware of the feeling of the
ground underneath her strange paws. The tickling of the
grass under her fur, rather than on her skin or clothes. It
was all strange but glorious.

The heightened senses were there, too, even ones she
wasn't aware of. A sixth sense, the animal instinct, she
supposed. She'd become aware of it when her bear had
helped her deftly avoid a poisonous snake hidden in the
tall grasses. Her head had snapped in its direction before
she saw, heard, or smelled anything, and she'd automati-

cally diverted her path, seeing only moments later the little serpent slither away.

But at least the regular excursions in the bear form ensured that the bear side wasn't overwhelming or distracting during the day, and she hadn't had another incident of waking up a bear.

And the more comfortable she became with her bear, the stronger the question was: *why* had her bear been locked up until now?

Sandy called her to let her know she'd made contact with an older bear shifter in the area who might be able to provide Jeanie with some information on her lineage. The woman wasn't attached to the pack, but she was an old friend of Sandy's and had agreed to meet with Jeanie.

Jeanie went by Ruby's to pick up some pastries on her way to visit the old bear.

"Hey, Jeanie," Ruby greeted her. "How's the bear working out for you?"

"If you're asking how badly I want that custom order of honey buns, honey-nut puff pastries, and honey wafers, the answer is extremely!"

Ruby laughed, but Jeanie noticed that her friend was acting a bit standoffish, keeping a few extra steps back from the counter and even avoiding eye contact. "Is everything okay?" Jeanie asked.

"It's fine, it's fine." Ruby slid the boxes across the counter while Jeanie handed over her debit card. "It's just, you know... you're a bear now."

"And?" Jeanie asked, not understanding the problem since she knew her raccoon shifter friend didn't judge others based on their animal type.

"I'm a raccoon," Ruby replied, crossing her arms over her chest and nervously rubbing her biceps. "Sometimes us prey-types have a natural aversion to the predator-types. It will just take a bit for my raccoon to get used to your bear. It got used to Sandy's wolf and plenty of others. It will just take time."

"Aww." Jeanie wanted to hug her friend but respected her space. She tried to move the conversation on and act like everything was normal, figuring that would be the best way to help her friend. "These snacks aren't all for me, though they smell good enough that I'm certain I could eat every last one. I'm off to have a chat with an older bear who might have some insight into all of this."

"Family?" Ruby asked, raising an eyebrow as she passed back Jeanie's card with her receipt.

"No, at least, I don't think she's family." The word rang in Jeanie's ear. She hadn't even thought about it. Leave it to Ruby—who'd been searching for her long-lost nieces—to hone in on that part of Jeanie's change. "Sandy would have mentioned if she'd suspected it."

"But you never know where it might lead," Ruby said with a hopeful smile. "Good luck!"

Jeanie's stomach rumbled the whole ninety-minute drive to Glynis Vire's home in the mountains. The pastry boxes smelled so good that it made Jeanie wonder if the woman would notice that there were only four or five of each instead of a half-dozen.

She was able to distract herself by what Ruby had mentioned: family.

Jeanie had been so focused on shifting, on learning to live with her bear, on being accepted into her pack, and sometimes on who might have been responsible for locking up her bear that she hadn't even thought about if she should try to find her *family.*

Her mother had raised her alone, informing her that her father had died before she was born and that his parents wanted nothing to do with either of them. Now Jeanie wondered, was it because Jeanie wasn't a bear? If she *had* been a bear, would she have been accepted into her father's side of the family?

And now that she *was* a bear, did she *want* to meet them?

She'd missed her mother every day since her mother died, but now more than ever, she wished her mother was still around so she could answer some of these questions.

When she arrived at the cabin, she grabbed the pastry boxes—still all full, miraculously—and stood nervously at Glynis's door, hesitant to knock. What might this woman tell Jeanie about her bear and maybe even her family? Was Jeanie ready to step through that door and enter an entirely new world of possibilities?

She didn't have to knock. The door swung open, and Jeanie set eyes on Glynis.

At over a hundred years old, Glynis had the number of wrinkles you'd expect. Her silver and white hair was short and brushed back, but her green eyes were piercing and revealed the intelligence behind them.

Her mouth wasn't quite turned up into a smile, but she didn't appear *unfriendly* either.

"Hello, Glynis. I'm Jeanie. Nice to meet you," she said,

juggling her purse and the pastry boxes so she could shake hands.

"Was the drive good?" Glynis's grip told Jeanie that the old woman had great strength hiding beneath her small, shriveled exterior.

"Yes, the roads were very clear." Jeanie stepped inside the cabin when Glynis gestured, slipping her shoes off at the door.

"All right, let me take a look at you," Glynis grunted and walked a circle around Jeanie, her walking stick punctuating the examination as though it were a clock, ticking away the seconds until judgment by this strange old woman.

Then Glynis leaned in close, sniffed Jeanie, and then locked eyes with her.

She nodded. Grunted again and said, "Bearstin."

"Oh. Bearstin." Jeanie nodded with no idea what that meant.

"Come on, sit down. Open up those boxes, and I'll get the tea."

Glynis's mouth finally turned into a smile when she looked over the treats Jeanie brought. "You have good taste."

"I've definitely been more interested in honey since becoming a bear."

"You didn't become a bear. You were born a bear," Glynis declared while pouring the hot water into the cups with tea bags.

"What makes you say that?" Jeanie asked.

"I've been around a few different older ones who were

made into shifters by science or magic," Glynis explained. "They have a different scent. A very distinct difference between a human smell and an animal smell, mixing with, almost an electric aura, if that makes sense to you"—she shrugged and handed Jeanie her cup—"in any case, you're a bear, you've always been a bear, but someone suppressed it."

"Do you know who?" Jeanie asked, jumping to conclusions.

"No," Glynis replied. "But it's obviously magic."

"How can you tell?"

"When one-hundred-two years old you become, many talents and powers you might have." Glynis laughed at her impersonation of Yoda, and Jeanie joined in while marveling at how well shifters are able to age, given their exceptional healing that gave them longer life spans. "I've been around long enough to recognize the lingering traces of magic on someone."

"So, Bearstin? What did you mean when you said that?"

Glynis nodded, chewing on a bite of honey bun and then swallowing. "Your family. You belong to the Bearstins. They're a bear sleuth not too far east of Georgetown. And you didn't know this, huh?"

"No, I didn't. My father died in an accident before I was born, and we never knew his family. They weren't married, and I just have my mother's name on my birth certificate."

"You never looked them up?"

"I tried. My mother told me his last name was Beanton." If Glynis was right—and Jeanie had no reason to doubt her—then it would explain why she'd never been able to track down that side of her lineage.

"Ah."

They chewed in silence for a moment.

"Why would my mother lie?"

"Why do you think the lie originated from your mother? Maybe your father gave her a false name."

Jeanie shrugged. "I don't know, but why would either of them lie?"

Glynis simply raised an eyebrow, allowing Jeanie to work through it on her own. "They're dangerous?"

Glynis shrugged, noncommittal. "I know the Bearstins. They're just your average bear sleuth. A bunch of fun-loving bears."

"So, then why?"

"Not all of them have always been so fun-loving." Glynis shook her head. "But I'm not a psychic. That's something you'll have to go there and find out for yourself."

"You sure it's Bearstin?" Jeanie confirmed, not wanting to drop in on a family and try to claim them if she didn't belong.

Glynis nodded. "I'm absolutely certain."

"I wonder if my mother knew he was a bear shifter."

Glynis's eyes grew wide. "Your mother was human?"

Jeanie nodded.

"Well, that could have something to do with it. Even forty years ago, some shifters weren't very accepting of non-shifters."

"So my father might have lied about his name, so she didn't know about the shifter family?"

Glynis shrugged. "Maybe."

"I feel like there is more you're not saying."

"This could be a master class in history and culture of bears and shifters because all we can do is make assumptions right now. I'm not going to make predictions. You will have to go to them and find all the answers you can from whoever is left."

"Left?"

"Whoever was around forty years ago who might have known your father. I can tell you that you're a Bearstin, but not why your mother didn't have you meet them. I know that you were born a bear and that some sort of magic kept the bear suppressed, but not who did it, why, or how."

They chatted for a bit longer. Glynis seemed more than happy to share her life story with Jeanie, and Jeanie felt she could talk to the woman for hours.

In fact, they did. Only when the afternoon sun started hitting her through Glynis's west-facing windows did Jeanie realize she better start heading home.

"Thank you, Glynis," Jeanie said, leaning in for a hug. "I'll call you and make a time to come back up if I learn more."

"Eh, don't worry about it," Glynis said, waving her hand away.

Jeanie smiled and shook her head. Someone as friendly as Glynis couldn't *really* hate visitors. She'd definitely be back for a visit. She wanted to hear more stories from Glynis. The old woman was undoubtedly a treasure trove of history.

The whole way home, though, Jeanie had a lot to

think about. Would she bother to go meet this unknown side of her family? Why *hadn't* she known them? Had her father or mother not wanted her to find that side of the family? If so, they had to have a good reason for that.

Should she respect their wishes and leave it alone? Maybe it was best to not open that Pandora's box.

But could she really live the rest of her life with that curiosity hanging there?

No, she didn't think so. Better go ahead and get it over with. The sooner, the better.

6

———————

AFTER DISCUSSING IT WITH OSCAR AND SANDY AND TAKING a few days to consider the pros and cons, Jeanie finally built up the courage to call the Bearstin number Sandy gave her.

The matriarch, Bliss Bearstin, proved to be beyond lovely. When Jeanie introduced herself as possibly a Bearstin, Bliss didn't become judgmental or doubtful like Jeanie had expected. Instead, Bliss instantly invited Jeanie to visit.

"She said they basically have a function every weekend. It's always a birthday or anniversary or some reason to gather together," Jeanie explained to Oscar while they prepared to leave the house and start the few-hour drive that Saturday.

Oscar chuckled. "Sounds like they like to party a bit more than our pack does."

"Maybe, or maybe it's just a centralized location, versus here in Georgetown where pretty much everyone is at one of the Mactire bars or clubs on the weekends."

"Everyone?" Oscar asked, risking moving near her, carefully avoiding her curling iron, to give her a kiss.

"Everyone young enough to still want to party, I guess." Jeanie laughed and waved him off. "Leave, or I'll never finish getting ready."

He was about to leave the bathroom, but she set down the curling iron and reached for him. He stopped, and she wrapped her arms around him in a hug.

"I'm not complaining, but what was that for?" he asked.

"You're being so supportive of this. Not just me becoming a bear, but you giving up a Saturday to meet a bunch of strangers."

"I'm not *giving up a Saturday*. My wife and I are just doing something different than usual."

She spent the whole car ride as a ball of nerves. This was different than just meeting new people. This was meeting a family she didn't know, and she didn't know *why* she didn't know them. Glynis and Sandy both had seemed confident that the Bearstins were good people, but what if they were wrong?

Or, what if they were right, but Jeanie embarrassed herself and made a bunch of nice people dislike her?

They finally pulled up to the home of Dan and Bliss Bearstin, the alpha and matriarch of the Bearstin bear sleuth.

"Holy cow, that's a lot of cars," Jeanie murmured while Oscar found a place to park.

Jeanie looked out toward the field behind the house and saw the already gathered crowd. Some people sat and talked, some stood around barbecues cooking and chatting, and many—adults and children—played yard games, from corn hole to ring toss and ladder ball to Kan Jam frisbee. The smaller kids jumped on a trampoline or pushed each other on tire swings

People of all ages gathered, from older than her age to even teens. She couldn't count the number of young kids running around since they seemed to be everywhere at once. She saw quickly that the little roly-poly bear children were clumsier and more into wrestling each other than the wolf children usually were—as they tended to like to play games like tag, running, jumping, and dodging in their playtime.

Jeanie couldn't help but grin while assessing the sea of smiles. She felt a little flutter in her stomach. From a first impression, they certainly *did* look friendly.

She left the car, and Oscar walked around to her side, taking her hand. "You ready?"

She nodded. "Let's do this."

They'd taken not a few steps before the welcome party arrived.

"Jeanie!" A tall, brown-haired, curvy woman called out and instantly enveloped Jeanie in a hug. "I'm Bliss, and this is my husband, Dan. You must be Oscar!"

Oscar was wrapped in a hug next while Dan—a tall, thick man with thinning brown hair and bushy eyebrows —shook Jeanie's hand. "Yes, you are a Bearstin," the alpha instantly assessed. "How curious."

Bliss waved her hands as though pushing the words away. "We have time to talk about that later. Right now, we're just getting to know each other. Come on, I'll introduce you to your long-lost family!"

One person after another welcomed her into the sleuth, all offering warm smiles and kind words. Jeanie had no chance of remembering all the names. The entire time, Jeanie couldn't stop wondering if the Bearstin sleuth was *really* good at hiding their dark side or if there was *no reason* her mother or father should have kept her from these people.

So why did they, then?

In no time, it was time to eat.

Meat and veggies piled off the barbecues, while bowls and plates of sides seemed to appear out of nowhere. A pile of plates and a big silverware bucket materialized on the lead table. The group of hungry bears waited while Bliss and Dan took their honored guests through the line first.

"Everyone of all ages come out to the big sleuth parties for endless food, drink, music—they'll pull out the instruments later," Bliss said once they'd sat at one of the picnic tables. "We like to call this the Rustic Bear Jamboree. Not to be confused with the very different 'country' version that is IP of a certain powerful mouse."

Jeanie laughed. "Well, it's good to know that party bears are alive and well."

"We sure are!" Bliss gave Jeanie and Oscar a moment to dig into their food before continuing. "We host one of these every weekend that we're not having an official sleuth meeting or another event. Even if I'm not here or Dan isn't here, our kids or another sleuth member takes over. We must have a consistent place people can come together."

"And even the teens show up," Jeanie said, gesturing to the crowded table of them. "That's impressive."

"It gives them all a place to grow up, to know each other, and have a feeling of belonging. Eventually, they start doing other things, but it's good for everyone to have a place to belong."

Jeanie felt the word *belong* like a stab to her heart. She should have belonged here, but it had been stolen from her.

Bliss saw Jeanie's face fall and touched her arm lightly. "You belonged here too. I don't know how you could have grown up with your bear suppressed, let alone not knowing we were here right around the corner from you, but know that Dan and I are determined to find your answers."

"And make up for lost time," Dan added with a wink. "Maybe we'll have to start doing two parties a week."

"You leave her alone," Bliss swatted at him before looking back at Jeanie. "You are absolutely welcome to every event you want to come to, but we're not going to pressure you to do more than you're comfortable with. You already have your own life, but however you decide to fit us into it, we'll be happy with it."

They stopped chatting to greet a new group that had just arrived and wanted to introduce themselves to Jeanie. Then, there was another group right behind them.

"Eat up. They'll leave you alone if your mouth is full," Bliss whispered.

When their plates were finally empty, they went back to chatting.

"Everything going on with me right now will be an

adjustment," Jeanie agreed. "But I really appreciate how welcoming you've all been."

"It will take time to warm up," Bliss said with a nod. "But I sure hope you do. We'd love you to come back."

"We will if you'll have us," Jeanie said.

Bliss wrapped her arm around Jeanie's shoulder, giving her a good squeeze and shoulder rub. "Good, because you're one of us, and we want to see more of you."

"You participate in the Mactire Pack events?" Dan asked, looking at both Oscar and Jeanie.

"Yes, sir, we do," Oscar said, showing reverence to the sleuth alpha. Even if Dan wasn't *his* alpha, he'd still show utmost respect to his position. "And while I have the chance, I wanted to make sure to thank you for inviting us out here. I know the situation is strange, but the welcome you're showing my wife is more than gracious."

"I can't believe there is this whole side to me that I missed out on," Jeanie mused. "I really don't understand why my mother would have denied me this, especially if she knew there was a chance I was a bear."

Bliss and Dan exchanged a look.

"We've been looking into it," Dan said. "See, the thing is, the sleuth is very careful about keeping track of children born to our members. The shifter secret isn't so hidden anymore, but back then, it certainly was. And our leadership has always been very good about tracking."

"So it doesn't make sense that they would not have checked in on you and your mother," Bliss finished.

"Maybe they didn't know about my mom and dad being together?" Jeanie suggested.

They shook their heads, and Dan explained, "We have records. Meticulous ones, kept by the sleuth historians. There is a record of your father announcing he was mated to a human."

"There was?" Jeanie asked, her heart leaping with excitement.

"We thought it best to speak to you about this in person, not over the phone," Bliss explained.

"Go on!" Jeanie urged, eager to learn everything she could about her parents and the sleuth.

"Your father announced he found his mate," Dan said. "And he introduced your mother to the sleuth. I'm sorry to say there was great upset from the more traditional members, which, at the time, outnumbered the more progressive-thinkers who were accepting of non-bears into the sleuth."

"What does that mean?" Jeanie asked.

A new woman's voice spoke up behind Jeanie. "It means they told your father he'd have to choose: his mate or his sleuth."

7

———

JEANIE TURNED. BEHIND HER STOOD A WOMAN WHO LOOKED to be of similar age to Glynis, if the number of wrinkles on her face was any indication. However, where Glynis had looked like a vibrant, rugged older lady, this woman seemed faded—wilted even—from her limp white bob to her sunken dull eyes.

"Hello, Edda. Come, sit down," Bliss invited, patting the edge of the bench beside her.

"All right," Edda said, though she acted like she'd rather be anywhere else.

Bliss turned back to Jeanie. "Bliss is our oldest sleuth member and the only one still around who was an adult back then and who knew the sleuth's leadership."

"And the records don't tell the whole story," Edda said, nodding and digging in after a young man placed a plate of food in front of her. "So they think they can pry into my brain for the missing information."

"Can they?" Jeanie asked, and Edda snapped her head over to look at her, assessing Jeanie.

After a moment of judgmental staring, Edda finally spoke again. "I met your mother."

A wave of shock hit Jeanie. Suddenly, everything became more real, as though until that moment, she'd just been play-acting a member of the Bearstins, but someone who'd really known her mother—and by extension, her father too? It was *real*.

"You did?" Jeanie asked, finding it hard to breathe.

"Yes," Edda confirmed. "She was a human who had a fling with a Bearstin member. Everyone talked about it. But like they"—Edda waved her hand in Bliss and then Dan's direction, a disrespectful gesture that shocked Jeanie— "said, we weren't as... *open* about humans coming into our sleuth back then."

Jeanie pressed her lips together and cast a glance at Oscar. Elders were highly esteemed in shifter communities, but that didn't mean the alpha and matriarch wouldn't be slighted by Edda's attitude. Jeanie noted to tread lightly so as not to insult any of the bears. "So what happened?"

"Your father had to leave the sleuth if he was going to be with your mother," Edda replied, her mouth full of soft foods the man had served her.

"Was he going to do it?" Jeanie asked.

"Yes." Edda shrugged, and then darkness passed over her face. "At least, that's what the consensus was—what we all thought he would do. We never really found out because then he was in that terrible construction accident that killed him."

Jeanie nodded. That much matched what her mother

had told her. At least not *everything* she'd been told had been a lie.

"Then your mother left," Edda continued. "We never heard from her again."

"She never told anyone she was pregnant? Not even my grandparents?"

Dan piped up. "The records indicate that members of the sleuth checked in with your mother for a year after your father's death. If those in charge knew she was pregnant at that time, they would have noted that, but there are no notes about a child."

"They knew about the child," Edda spat angrily, making little pieces of chewed-up barbecue fly and causing Bliss to discretely wipe her arm. "They just didn't record it because they were confident the child wasn't a bear, so it wouldn't be of concern to the sleuth."

"Is this *true*, Edda?" Bliss asked gently, offering Edda a fresh napkin.

"Why would I lie?" Edda bit back, snatching the cloth from Bliss.

"I'm not saying you would, Edda," Bliss calmly replied. "But sometimes we get carried away with stories and—"

"I'm not telling a tale!" Edda interrupted. "This is what happened."

"Then do you know why they were confident that the baby wasn't a bear?" Dan prodded.

"When I heard about it, I figured that the child just didn't present as a bear," Edda said after a few more bites. "I thought, oh, great, the sleuth really dodged a bullet there. Except for losing your father." Edda looked at

Jeanie, and her eyes seemed to soften. "That was tragic. It nearly killed your grandparents. There was talk about letting them know about the baby, that maybe it would help them through the grieving, but ultimately they decided not to."

"It *would* have helped them," Bliss said.

"Not if the shame of having their genes in a non-shifter would have been too great," Edda shrugged as though she wasn't delivering news that hurt Jeanie to her core. "That's what I'd assumed at first, anyway, but now I see there was more to it. They didn't want anyone around that baby because *someone* would have sniffed out that there was a bear in there, even if suppressed somehow."

"You think they suppressed it?" Jeanie asked, her voice raw.

Edda shrugged and avoided eye contact. Jeanie thought Edda knew more, but the old woman wasn't offering it.

"This isn't our way," Dan muttered. "Leadership wouldn't have done that. They would have taken in the mother and the child, shifter or not—full of hatred toward non-shifters or not."

"Not if the mother refused." Edda shrugged.

"My mother refused?"

"How should I know? I'm just telling you what we all figured." Edda's plate was clean now, and she waved to the young man. "Well, dinner was satisfactory. I'm going home now."

Jeanie watched in horror as the young man helped Edda to her feet and walked her away from the party. She wanted to ask more questions, but she knew the shifter rule —as in any polite society, really—was to respect the elders. Dan, as her alpha, *could* have commanded she stay and tell them more, but he was honoring her position as an elder by allowing her to make her own choices of what to share.

"We'll follow up with her," Bliss promised, clearly seeing how much it upset Jeanie to have Edda leave on that note.

Jeanie nodded.

"And don't take anything Edda says to heart," Bliss said. "They were a little gruffer back then, and Edda's never outgrown that."

"I understand," Jeanie murmured, telling herself she couldn't hold it against Edda. She was just the messenger. She wasn't the one who orchestrated what had been done to Jeanie. She thought back on all that Edda said. "So, they gave my father an ultimatum? Does that sound likely to you?"

Dan nodded. "I'm aware that often happened back then. If their mate was human, they could leave and be with their mate and without a sleuth, or reject them and know they would be un-mated—no partner, no kids—for life."

"A lone bear forever, either way," Jeanie concluded. "All because someone made the rules that they wouldn't allow human mates, when really, how ridiculous because *fate* said a human mate is okay, but *they* thought they knew better?"

She was getting worked up, and Oscar placed his hand on hers. She met his eyes. He was always her rock when the waters turned choppy. She had to restrain her fury now so she didn't insult the Bearstins.

She took a deep, calming breath and turned back to Dan. "The records don't say anything else?"

"The records wouldn't keep something like that, like hiding a bear. It notes nothing about a child, and there is no more mention of your mother."

Jeanie heard the sound of strings tuning and turned to see that just as Bliss had promised, several sleuth members had brought out instruments. Guitars, fiddles, and even a banjo.

"I think maybe I just need to absorb all this information for now," Jeanie surmised.

Bliss nodded. "Just remember, this isn't over. We're going to keep looking into this and find your answers."

For the next little while, the bears laughed and danced and sang, and before she knew it, hours had passed, and Jeanie yawned. Bliss had informed her that the party would be going well after midnight. No one would blame them for leaving early, especially considering their long drive.

Deciding it was a good time to leave, they thanked Bliss and Dan for the hospitality again and assured them that they had a good time.

Oscar drove home in the darkness while Jeanie rode quiet and contemplative.

"You think we'll go back?" she asked.

"Of course, we will," he answered. "Why would you even ask?"

"They're all very nice, yes, but something doesn't feel

right. Someone didn't want me there. Someone *hid* even my birth from the sleuth, not just my bear from me."

"Exactly, someone hid you from them, which means you shouldn't punish *them* any further. Whoever orchestrated this is long gone."

"Except for Edda," Jeanie pointed out.

"Edda doesn't know anything," Oscar said.

"Why do you sound so certain?"

"Because she's not a bear of any position, and the packs and sleuths used to be wilder back then. Meaner."

"And more patriarchal," Jeanie concluded. "Meaning they wouldn't have let women in on taking care of stuff like this—like *me*—back then."

"Exactly. Involve a woman in matters involving a baby, and undoubtedly their bleeding hearts would fold." Oscar nudged her elbow with his playful tease. "Now, no more questioning if you'll go back. They're your family, and whether you know it or not, your heart is already holding them. It's better to live a life where you embrace all the love they have to give and give it back to them."

He was right. Jeanie's heart had already grown that night.

8

———

The following weekend, Jeanie went back to Ruby's to pick up another order of honey treats before she visited with Glynis.

Ruby asked Stephanie to work the counter and sat with Jeanie at one of the small tables in the bakery, which Jeanie took to be an excellent sign: Ruby's raccoon wasn't so nervous around her anymore.

Jeanie listened, shocked, while Ruby filled her in on all the excitement having to do with Ruby's three missing nieces.

"So you found them!"

"Yes, we found each other." Ruby smiled, and her face lit up in a way Jeanie hadn't seen since before Ruby's brother had died a few years ago. "And you? How did your meeting with your long-lost family go?"

Jeanie took a breath. "I've been trying to sort out my feeling on it. Don't get me wrong, everyone I met—well, mostly everyone I met—was *really nice*. It's just this whole *why they didn't want me* thing, and why they would suppress the shifter powers of a *baby*."

"It's rough," Ruby agreed. "Only really dark, dangerous witches are willing to put curses on the innocent."

"You think that's it?" Jeanie asked. "A dark witch?"

"I can't imagine what else it would be."

"Me neither."

The doors opened, and in poured a bunch of people. *Rabbits,* Jeanie thought, and the idea shocked her. She'd never been able to identify other shifters before, and that's what she was doing, right? "Are they the reason you have all the carrot options now?"

Ruby smiled and blushed. "I guess I haven't told you about Paul and his rabbit family, huh?"

"No!" Jeanie cried. "Girl, you owe me a dinner date, stat! Well, unless you're too occupied with this, *Paul* fellow—"

"I'll work you in, I promise!"

"I'm holding you to it!"

Ruby went off to provide the rabbits with their treats, and Jeanie took her boxes of honey snacks to her car and headed off on her drive to follow up with Glynis.

When she'd called to schedule a time to visit, Glynis had tried to tell her to just give her the info over the phone, stating there was no need to make a trip, but Jeanie refused. She had the distinct impression that a bit of company now and again *was* something Glynis enjoyed.

"You're back," Glynis stated when Jeanie knocked on the door.

"Of course, I'm back," Jeanie replied with a shake of her head, stepping in and taking off her shoes. "I called and *told* you I would visit today."

"Doesn't mean you'd actually do it," Glynis replied, clearly in a bit of a grumpy mood. Jeanie wondered if it had something to do with Glynis being anxious to learn all the details of the Bearstin visit. "What'd you bring?"

"More honey treats from Ruby's."

"Well, at least there's that." Glynis gestured Jeanie toward the living room while she shuffled to the stove, where she heated up the kettle.

"Let me get that for you," Jeanie offered.

"I can do it myself just fine." Glynis gave Jeanie a little shove toward the living room. "If I can't so much as make tea, then I have no business being out here living alone."

"Well, I'm at least getting the plates for the sweets," Jeanie turned back and headed to the cabinet. This time, Glynis didn't fight her.

When they finally sat, each with a plate of treats and a cup of tea, Jeanie filled Glynis in on the visit, starting with the warm welcome they'd all given her.

"I'm so glad I don't have to go to things like that anymore," Glynis said with a huff.

"Are you really, though?" Jeanie asked. "It seems so... lonely living out here by yourself."

"Don't go feeling bad for me," Glynis replied. "Undoubtedly, yes. I prefer to live my life like this. I'd lose my mind having to deal with people all the time. The occasional visitor"—Glynis waved her hand toward Jeanie—"is tolerable, maybe. So long as I have time to myself in between."

"Didn't you grow up in a sleuth?"

"Why all these questions about me? I'm not the interesting one here. What did they say about your father and mother?"

The old woman listened attentively, and by the time Jeanie finished, Glynis had started smiling, confirming that her earlier grumpiness *was* because she was anxious about the story.

Jeanie was glad she'd decided to visit in person. It was worth it to see Glynis's pleased face.

"Well, I'm glad I was able to send you in the right direction."

"Thank you for that," Jeanie said.

Glynis waved her hand, staring at her food while working through her thoughts. "Anyway, all you learned was that the bears back then lied about your existence."

"Omitted it," Jeanie corrected with a shrug.

"Regardless, someone hateful—or *someones* hateful—not only knew about you, but made sure your bear wouldn't emerge, and then either made the records say there was no child or filled in the historian with that false information."

Jeanie nodded. "That's about all we can come up with, yep."

Glynis's thoughtful mien turned toward Jeanie for a moment. "You know, don't let what happened back then affect how you feel about the sleuth now. Things really *have* changed since the old days, when more shifters hated humans—sure, *some* still do hate humans, but it's so much more common now for shifters to mate with humans and take them into the sleuth or pack."

"Yes, I suppose that's true."

"The Mactires never had a problem with you, right? Accepted you when you were human and still accept you now that you're a bear."

"Yes, that's correct."

"So that means the bears accept you too."

Jeanie sighed and dropped her head in her hands. "This is all supposed to be over with. I'm settled into midlife."

"And I'm supposed to be settled into old age, yet people like you are still showing up on my door, disrupting my peace."

Jeanie smiled at that. "Well, that's because you don't need to just lock yourself up and fade away. We have to shake things up for you because you deserve better than to live alone."

"You mean die alone," Glynis countered, finishing the last bite of her pastry and then wiping her fingers on the lace napkin. She stood, closed the treat boxes, and moved the tea kettle back to the kitchen.

Jeanie helped her, though she wasn't sure why Glynis was quickly wrapping up their visit.

"So, no records," Glynis said, allowing Jeanie to wash the plates.

"Nope."

"And Edda just got up and left without coming out with all she knows."

She said the woman's name as though she knew exactly who she was. Jeanie guessed she probably did. "Yeah. Dan and Bliss said they'd follow up with her, but you know how it is. It would have been out of line to stop her from leaving."

"You needed someone her own age there."

"They said she was the oldest member of the sleuth."

"I'm older." Glynis laughed. "Now, get your shoes on. We're going."

"Going where?"

Glynis grabbed her coat, hat, and handbag and said, "You're driving me to Edda Bearstin's house."

9

———————

"Are you a Bearstin?" Jeanie asked while she drove, following Glynis's directions.

Not only did Glynis seem to *know* Edda, but she even knew where she lived.

"Nope," Glynis answered. "I'm not a Bearstin, but I know them. I'm old enough to know practically everyone, at least in the area. But I have a long history with Edda."

"True as that may be, I have to call Bliss and let her know we're heading there. I can't let the sleuth think I'm going over their alpha's head to get information from Edda."

"Smart bear." Glynis nodded and stayed silent while Jeanie used her hands-free device in her car to call Bliss.

Jeanie reasoned that Bliss would at least understand that she was in no position to deny Glynis's request to take her to Edda's.

When they arrived, the Bearstin matriarch was already parked on the corner of Edda's street.

Glynis didn't stop to make pleasantries with Bliss,

simply gave her a nod and walked up to Edda's front door, her cane clacking on the concrete the whole way.

"How are you doing?" Bliss asked, putting her arm around Jeanie's shoulder while Glynis pounded on the front door.

"I hope I haven't caused more problems," Jeanie mumbled. "I wanted to update Glynis since she was the one who directed me to you, and then she insisted on this, and I guess I should have refused, but—"

"You can't refuse an old bear." Bliss laughed. "It's one of the perks of our senior years we get to look forward to!"

Hmm, Jeanie thought. She'd never imagined herself being a pack elder, a status reserved only for shifters in packs and sleuths. Now, she would be. It was a new idea.

Edda opened her front door and surveyed the guests on her porch. "I'm sorry," she said, her voice full of false sweetness that even Jeanie could detect. "If I'd known I would be expecting visitors, I would have cleaned up or made sure to have refreshments. Maybe you all could return another—"

"Cut the crap, Edda," Glynis said, sticking her cane in the door's crack when Edda tried to close it. "Let us in."

The two old women stared at each other for a long time, and finally, Edda relented and opened the door. Glynis walked through the house like she'd been there many times, leading Jeanie and Bliss to the sitting room.

Edda, as promised, didn't offer them refreshments, but she did at least paint a sweet smile on her face. "What can I do for you, ladies?"

"You know why we're here. Finish telling us what you

know about what happened to the girl," Glynis said, motioning toward Jeanie.

Edda blinked in fake confusion. "I told them what I know. Did my information not help Dan and Bliss find more? It *is* their job to do that, isn't it?"

Her words were a slight at the leadership, but Bliss took it in stride. "We have looked into the situation some more and found no answers. Honestly, I'm at a loss here. I just can't fathom why it was of any benefit to try to block people from our sleuth. To try to keep the sleuth some kind of exclusive club. Love spreads. It's endless. The more, the merrier!"

"That's what's wrong with the sleuth today, that kind of thinking," Edda spat. "You shouldn't even be the leader. You and your husband are too soft on things like this—accepting outsiders."

"No, ma'am," Bliss objected. "Jeanie isn't an *outsider*. She's every bit one of us."

"If you want to live a life without *outsiders*"—Glynis added, saying the word as though it were poison on her tongue—"then you can choose to live a life like I do. Away from everyone. But you wanna be in a sleuth, then you don't get a choice about who's born or married into it."

"Why did you even come here today?" Edda asked, avoiding eye contact with all of them. "I told you all I know."

"Spit it out!" Glynis commanded, and Edda drew into herself, looking smaller and frailer than before.

Jeanie looked at Bliss. Clearly, whatever else Edda knew, she wasn't comfortable talking about it.

"What good is it to hide the knowledge you have?" Bliss asked, her voice gentle as she coaxed Edda to talk. "Are you protecting someone? Yourself?"

"*I* didn't do it!" Edda hurriedly defended herself, but once the words were out, they all knew she had more information than she'd shared.

"Edda, do you have tea in the kitchen?" Jeanie asked, figuring it would give Edda a few moments to collect herself. "Maybe Bliss and I can make some to help settle your nerves. Glynis and I brought some snacks too. I can go get those."

Edda nodded, and Bliss headed toward the kitchen while Jeanie ran back to her car. When she returned, she heard Glynis and Edda speaking in low tones to each other but couldn't make out the words. She figured Glynis was saying whatever it took to make Edda tell them the truth.

She helped Bliss gather the cups and tea, and Bliss poured the water. They found sugar and milk and prepared the tea as the women requested.

When they finally all had drinks and snacks, Edda took a steadying breath.

"Maybe I *heard* that there used to be a certain witch you could go to, who could take care of *certain* problems long ago. I think she cursed too many people, ended up on the wrong person's bad side, and got chased out of town many years ago. I don't want to talk about it because everyone else who knows about the witch is dead. And I don't want to be dead."

"We're all going to die eventually," Glynis said with a shake of her head.

"I mean, I don't want to become the witch's target!" Edda cried. "I've kept my mouth shut all these years and stayed safe."

"Do you know this witch?" Bliss asked. "Her name, where she is?"

"No. I don't know her name or where she is now. I don't know anyone who knows *of* her either."

"Does she know of you?" Jeanie asked. "If you're worried about her coming after you—"

"No, I don't think she knows about me," Edda interrupted. "But if you're somehow able to find her, all she has to do is look back to who is the old bear in the sleuth and figure out it was me running my mouth!"

Jeanie turned to Bliss and Glynis. "Why would the bear awaken now, though? Was the curse only supposed to last forty years?"

"Could be," Glynis answered. "Or it could be someone found a way to undo her enchantments."

"Or she did it herself to unleash chaos," Bliss added. "Or maybe someone wronged her, and she broke the enchantment out of vengeance."

"Why isn't anyone wondering if maybe she just had a change of heart?" Jeanie asked.

The three other women laughed. "Even if she *did* have a change of heart," Bliss explained. "There's nothing altruistic about dropping this kind of thing on someone's life."

Jeanie peered at Edda closely. "You're sure you don't know who she is or where she is? This witch?"

But Edda seemed to be telling the truth about that much. "I don't."

"Who went to the witch about Jeanie?" Bliss asked.

Edda shrugged. "I can assume, just as you can, that it wouldn't have been done by leadership, but perhaps by some others who... took care of little sleuth messes. Back then, if you needed certain favors, witches were around and more than willing to do a charm, enchantment, or curse... so long as you had just the right payment. Keeping the scales balanced and all that."

Bliss's face turned horrified, and Glynis just nodded grimly, like Edda was confirming a suspicion she already had.

"What?" Jeanie asked.

Glynis answered. "Whoever put the curse on you bargained with your father's life. Either the accident wasn't really an accident, or it's not actually how he died at all."

"That can't be!" Jeanie objected. "A witch would take his life?"

"And only a sleuth member of high standing would have the power to give that life to the witch in exchange for the curse," Edda said.

Bliss objected. "No. No way any member of our sleuth would authorize the death of another bear, no matter what. Not even if they were leaving the sleuth. It is absolutely unthinkable and wouldn't have happened."

"I doubt they understood they sentenced her father to death," Edda shrugged. "Witches are trickly like that."

"What kind of witch deals in *life force*?" Jeanie asked.

"A very bad one," Glynis answered.

"Wouldn't this witch have gotten a reputation?" Jeanie asked. "Wouldn't more people know about her?"

"No, the underground of the shifter world can be very dark and mysterious," Bliss answered. "Hence, if she angered the wrong person, she would have been run out of town; otherwise, they would have killed her, and no one would have known."

"And she's now getting revenge by breaking the curses?"

They shrugged.

"Why don't you know more details?" Jeanie asked Edda. "The witch's name, who did this to me, stuff like that?"

Edda shrugged. "I have a big mouth, always did. So no one told me anything. I know all I do just from listening while going unnoticed. All that other important stuff, no one let me in on."

Jeanie looked to Bliss for confirmation. "She's not lying. She was never leadership, never high-ranking. I'll talk to Dan, though, and see if he knows anything."

"I might know one thing," Edda reluctantly admitted. "I know the location of her old shop."

10

BLISS INSISTED ON DRIVING, SO THEY ALL PILED INTO HER car for the drive a few towns over.

Jeanie thought that Georgetown had a cozy vibe, and in contrast, this town had more of a historic feel. The buildings were old but well-maintained, with little historical plaques on nearly every building.

Edda directed them to the downtown square and pointed out an antique shop at the very edge, butted up to a tree line that split downtown and a large open-space park.

"From what I understand, she used to run this store," Edda explained. "It was a good front."

"Did you ever meet her? Go shopping here?" Jeanie asked.

Edda shook her head. "Never."

Bliss found them a parking spot right in front of the location Edda indicated.

Jeanie, Bliss, and Glynis all piled out of the car, but Edda hesitated.

"She really is scared, isn't she?" Jeanie asked Bliss, wondering if she should feel the same amount of fear.

"Leave the car, you old bat!" Glynis called to Edda.

Edda shook her head, and Glynis stomped over to the other side of the car and wrenched the door open.

"I don't understand why the three of you aren't worried about becoming the witch's target!" Edda cried. "She suppressed the girl's bear. What if she does that to all of us for interfering? Or worse?"

"It doesn't work like that," Glynis said, wrenching Edda out of the car. "Now, let's go."

"I don't know why I have to even be here," Edda muttered. "I told you all I know. I'm of no use past telling you this location."

"It's an adventure," Glynis replied. "How many more of these you gonna get in your life?"

Edda continued to gripe, but Jeanie tuned her out, looking at the store. There was no sign indicating if it was opened or closed or what the store hours were. The windows displayed many different items, from vases to dinnerware, to books and lamps. The density of the items suggested the place wasn't abandoned.

"I guess we try to go in?" Jeanie suggested, noticing that everyone had halted on the sidewalk, a good two feet from the building.

Bliss nodded but didn't move.

Jeanie tried to move one foot in front of the other, but every inch of her being refused.

"It's warded," Glynis said. "You can feel the magic in the air. She clearly didn't want people nosing around."

"Exactly what we're doing," Edda complained.

"How do we pass the wards?" Jeanie asked.

Glynis shrugged and took a step forward. "You just accept that it's going to feel real bad, and just do it."

Jeanie finally stepped forward and felt a rush of disgust and fear wash over her.

Bliss followed, but Edda did not.

"Just leave her for now," Bliss said.

"Can I help you, ladies?" A man with buzz-cut hair wearing slacks and a checkered button-up shirt appeared from around the corner of the building and slowly approached them with a warm smile on his face.

"We're just sightseeing," Bliss replied.

The man looked at the four of them. "Well, the best coffee place is just around the corner."

"We're interested in antiques," Jeanie said, gesturing to the building.

"It's not open," he quickly replied. "The owners are out of town this week."

Jeanie nodded, wondering if he was telling the truth or if he was lying for the witch for some reason. "Oh, so you think it will be open next week?"

"He's a watchdog," Glynis said before the man could answer. "Don't bother talking to him. He's not real."

"He looks solid enough to me," Edda muttered.

"Solid doesn't mean real," Glynis clarified. "He's probably a golem."

"Is he going to attack us if we don't listen to him?" Jeanie wrung her hands in worry.

"Doubtful. Not out here in the open, anyway. If the witch left something dangerous over here, it would have drawn attention long ago."

"Don't the townspeople notice that this place is never open?"

"It's glamoured," Glynis explained. "It probably looks like it's open to people."

"What if they try to go inside?"

"The wards probably turn most people around. They get the icky feeling and decide not to go in, and then Mr. Watchdog shows up and directs them elsewhere."

"How do you know all this stuff about magic?" Jeanie wondered.

Glynis shrugged. "I like to read a lot."

"Okay, because I'm starting to get the feeling that you know so much because you're actually the witch, and you're going to turn on us." Jeanie laughed nervously, partially joking but also slightly concerned by Glynis's wealth of knowledge on magic.

Glynis rolled her eyes and shook her head. "If I were the witch, then Edda would have been more scared of *me*."

"True enough," Jeanie agreed, putting the thought aside. Glynis had helped her thus far, and it was true that, though there was animosity between Glynis and Edda, the latter didn't seem afraid of Glynis.

They ignored the watchdog, who continued to tell them of various local points of interest and restaurants, and Jeanie reached for the door handle.

"Locked."

She tried knocking, and no one answered.

"We'll have to break in, I guess..." Jeanie said, though she already feared what breaking and entering might lead to.

"That would draw attention." Glynis looked around them, back toward the street. Though there weren't any other pedestrians—besides Mr. Watchdog—there were cars passing every once in a while.

"Let's look for a back entrance," Bliss suggested, and Edda moaned.

"Or let's just give this up."

"We're already here. We're going to find whatever we can." Glynis pushed Edda forward, and the group walked around the building.

To Jeanie's relief, the watchdog stayed at the front.

The wards, on the other hand, only seemed to get stronger.

They found the back door with concrete steps leading up to it. The loading dock had long since crumbled.

"I'm guessing the witch did some kind of magic to make the trees tear up the back road?" Jeanie asked, seeing how there was no longer enough room between the building and the woods for trucks to come in.

"Seems that way," Glynis replied. "Shall we?"

Bliss took the lead, and the moment her first foot hit the steps, they were greeted by a series of growls coming from the woods.

The women spun.

Behind them, they found four bears of differing colors stepping out from the trees.

"An enchantment," Edda sighed. "It summoned a foe for each of us."

Bliss, Glynis, and even Edda began stripping. Jeanie looked at them in shock.

"Better take your clothes off if you want to be able to

wear them later," Bliss explained. "Otherwise, you'll be naked or wearing shredded duds."

"What?" Jeanie blinked, shocked still. "I can't shift into a bear and *fight!* I've never done that before!"

"Do I have to tell you there's a first time for everything?" Glynis snapped.

"Why? Why don't we ignore them?" Jeanie protested.

"Too late now," Edda, who Jeanie expected to be the most likely to suggest running at a time like this, said. "Once we've been targeted with a spell like this, we have no choice. It will follow you back to Georgetown if you don't deal with it now."

Once again, Jeanie wondered how the older women understood so much about magic that she didn't. At least Bliss—and Sandy, too, for that matter— had seemed to not know much more than Jeanie had. Maybe their generation, in general, had been more concerned about magic. Were the witches evil back then? Meaning, they had to be more on alert for magic that might target them? That would make sense. They had to know about magic so they could protect themselves.

It wasn't time to think about that now, though. Jeanie stripped and barely had to think about her bear—it was ready to emerge and fight!

"I'm guessing they'll be activated once we breach the entrance," Bliss said in Jeanie's mind.

"Wait, why are you in my pack link?" Once again, Jeanie's mind pushed her to look at the more minor points than the big, snarling ones she literally faced.

"Because you're a Bearstin," Edda snapped in the link. Jeanie snuck a glance at Glynis, who seemed blissfully

unaware of the discussion while she stood her ground against the magical version of herself. She wasn't a Bearstin, so she wasn't privy to the mental conversation the three others now had.

"How are we going to face magic versions *of us?"* Jeanie asked. *"I don't understand how you beat magic."*

"It's meant to attack you if you breach the door. All you have to do is fight it until it weakens and disappears. You're not killing anything. You're just battling the magic that's targeted on you."

"Wait, we're not totally screwed until you breach *the door? Maybe let's not breach the door then!"*

"Jeanie!" Bliss's voice in her head was a commanding tone that somehow made her feel the need to listen and follow orders. She recognized it as part of Bliss's matriarch powers. *"Pretend it's a new workout routine or something, okay? Punch-punch, kick-kick, snarl, bump, tackle, whatever until the magic disappears, okay? Just do it!"*

So far, Jeanie had gone along on the witch hunt, perfectly unaware of any real dangers they might face, and only now did she stop to wonder if it was a bad idea. Now she really wished she'd just stayed home and let the mystery of the witch go.

It didn't matter. She was there now, and she had to do what she had to do. Bliss took the lead, busting down the glamoured door. Sure enough, the moment it opened, the four guardians attacked.

11

The other women engaged their foes in blurs, grappling, roaring, and biting.

Jeanie looked warily at the opposing brown bear, who was slowly walking toward her, its head down as it made low bellowing sounds. She'd not spent any time looking at herself in her bear form, so she only knew it must look like her based on how the others looked like Jeanie's friend's animals.

If it's my mirror, will it mirror behavior too? She took a few steps back, hoping her opponent would do the same.

Nope, it wasn't that kind of mirror magic. The brown bear looked like her but didn't act like her, and it kept walking forward.

She had to fight it.

Panic coursed through her. She didn't know how to fight—she'd never been in a physical altercation before.

Her foe didn't care. It reared up on its hind legs and then smashed down on top of her, knocking her to the ground and then pummeling her with punch after punch.

Jeanie tried to push the bear off, tried to get in some blows, but she was uncoordinated, and she was also too terror-stricken to figure out what she needed to do.

Let bear side guide you.

It was there, begging her to let go of control, but Jeanie still held onto her fear that if she let it have the reins, it wouldn't hand them back.

Her opponent continued to attack, and when it bit down on Jeanie's neck, she let out a huge roar of pain.

Let bear take over.

No, I can do this. Bliss said punch-punch, kick-kick, that's all I have to do.

She managed to knock the bear off her neck and roll away, but it was right behind her as she got to her feet, taking a swipe at her backside.

Jeanie felt the claws scratch through her tough hide, and she roared again in pain.

Turning to face the enemy, she knew she couldn't do it.

I can't do this. I can't fight a bear!

She'd been raised her whole life to know not to mess with bears. They were huge and strong, and humans had no chance against them.

You're not human. You're bear! Her animal side reminded her. *Stop the useless human thinking and let bear out!*

She was still too scared.

Are you more scared of outside bear, who wants to hurt you, or inside bear, who wants to save you?

The enemy grappled with her, shoving her to the ground again.

She felt her bear side tug at her, and she knew she no longer had a choice.

Help me.

The moment she opened up to it, all her human fear and overthinking faded, and she simply moved on instinct. Her bear knew exactly what to do, guiding her body to fight the enemy, blocking blows, and getting her own in.

She would have marveled at it, but there was no room to think.

She simply moved. Dodged. Attacked.

As she advanced, the bear she fought started to fade and weaken, but it didn't let up. It still fought her just as fiercely, though she felt her own strength fading.

"It's all about stamina," Bliss told her through the pack link. *"Just keep going."*

Jeanie roared, using Bliss's encouragement to help push her through.

Another grapple, another swing, a final tackle!

And the magical bear doppelganger finally vanished.

She panted, catching her breath while she stared at the spot where her foe had just been.

Had that all really happened?

Jeanie turned, and the three others—who'd all already finished fighting their foes, shifted, and changed—clapped for her.

Jeanie shifted back into her human form, asking, "Uh, you guys couldn't have helped me?"

"Nope," Glynis answered, not at all panting like Jeanie

was, though her cheeks were flushed and her smile bigger than Jeanie had ever seen. "You had to do it yourself. Good job, newbie."

Bliss ran toward her with a pocket-size first-aid kit in hand. "I never leave home without one," she explained as she started dabbing Jeanie's wounds with a cleaning wipe that stung.

Jeanie saw the others had some bandages on as well. "Is everyone okay?"

"We're all fine," Bliss assured her. "And you are too. You have shifter healing now. The bandages are more of a placebo kind of thing. It gives your human brain the signal that you're all patched up. Meanwhile, your bear is making sure you're fixed up in no time."

Bliss helped her wipe off the blood where the magic bear had bit and scratched her and applied a few bandages to the worst of the cuts. Then, Jeanie dressed and joined the others near the building's back entry.

"We'll need to be careful going in," Glynis cautioned. "We've gotten through her wards, her watchdog, and now her protectors. Guaranteed she has more inside."

They took step after careful step through the building's main floor, but they sprung no traps.

They fanned out, looking for anything that might tell them something about the store's owner, but all they found were antiques covered in layers of dust. Behind the checkout counter, there was nothing. No sales sheets, no business cards. The office was the same.

The witch had really cleaned it all out.

They checked out the basement next, finding it to be a second level of antiques—mainly large furniture items.

Even checking all the drawers of the desks and dressers turned up no clues. If they hadn't faced all the magic outside the building, Jeanie might think they were just in an ordinary antique shop.

"Should we look for secret doors or anything?" Jeanie asked.

"I doubt she'd have them in an area the public went," Glynis answered.

"She sure knows a lot about witches," Jeanie muttered to Bliss.

Bliss only raised an eyebrow and mouthed, "I know, weird, right?"

Glynis harrumphed, "I told you, I'm just knowledgeable."

Finally, the last place to look was upstairs.

Again, they cautiously took the stairs, expecting traps and finding none.

"Why would she set so much protection outside but not inside?" Jeanie asked the resident witch experts.

"*Time* would be my guess," Glynis answered. "She wouldn't have had traps in the part of her store that is open to the public—bad for business if her customers were triggering them—and if she had to get out of town quickly, she probably did what she could and that didn't include time for indoor traps."

The stairs ended at a locked door, which Bliss didn't hesitate to bust down again. Jeanie braced herself for another encounter with the mirror animals—as had happened with the last door knocked down—but none appeared.

"This is her apartment," Glynis concluded when they walked in.

"Obviously," Jeanie replied sarcastically, looking at the couch, the kitchen off to the side, and the door ajar that revealed a bed.

Glynis gave her a small rap with her cane. "Yes, obviously, it's an apartment. What I meant was that the same magic throughout this room is the same that lingers on you."

"What does that mean?"

"It's the witch's magic fingerprints," Edda explained. "Our bears can smell it. It was inside you with her enchantment, and it's all over this place. Was probably outside with the wards, too, but we didn't notice until being *in* her place."

Magic fingerprints? Jeanie shuddered. The idea put images of the witch putting her evil hands all over Jeanie's brain—or heart, whichever held the key to her bear.

At least the thought made her feel less guilty about digging through the witch's private drawers and cabinets.

Though once again, they found everything empty. Not a single trace. No photograph so they could say, "Hey, there she is!" No magical components that would let them say, "Ah, yes, we know who used these!" Nothing.

When the witch left, she cleared it all out.

"Then why ward the place outside? Set so many guards?" Jeanie asked.

"Because no one wants people snooping around their place, simple," Glynis replied.

"But why does she want this place? Why hold onto it?"

"That's not a bad question," Bliss replied, though no one seemed to know the answer to it.

They took one last look around. As Jeanie walked through the bathroom, she thought she saw something flicker in the mirror. Thinking it was just a trick of her eyes, she blinked and then looked again.

Before her eyes, the mirror rippled, and a voice emerged.

"How dare you enter my home," it hissed.

"Who are you? Are you the witch whose place this is?" Jeanie spoke loudly, so her friends could hear her and come running.

"Who else? And I know you're not alone. I know you have friends with you."

"We want to know who you are."

A cackle sounded from the rippling mirror. "Is that all? You sure you're not also wanting to ask me *where* I am?"

"I want to know why you cursed babies forty years ago and why those curses are being undone now!"

The mirror hesitated before replying. "Who are *you*?"

"One of the babies you cursed."

The mirror cackled again. "Well, I expected my old customers to come looking for me. I didn't anticipate those cursed to look too. Or rather, I hadn't thought they'd find me."

"I want to know who bargained with you to curse me!" Jeanie shouted, unleashing the rage that had been slowly simmering since the day she turned into a bear.

"And how many more people are affected by your curse? Will they all be experiencing what I did?"

Bliss, Glynis, and Edda had gathered at the bathroom door, looking in with a mixture of surprise, shock, and horror as Jeanie screamed at the magical mirror.

The mirror was silent. Jeanie expected her to not answer. But then the witch behind the mirror spoke. "Why don't you pull up some chairs and let me tell you all about it..."

Years ago—forty to fifty years, but who's counting?—I was just a young witch, trying to fit in. I dreamed of a normal life. Marriage, kids. Owning a little antique shop. Having friends.

Being accepted.

But that dream was too big. Whereas I thought that a town full of shifters would be a perfect place for another paranormal to fit in, that was not the case.

Back then, there was so much elitism. If you weren't born into a proper witch family, you weren't accepted into the covens. It was much the same with shifters, as you know. Nowadays, the shifter groups take in whomever, and witches can apply for sponsorship to covens.

But I had no such options when I was first on my own.

Not only did I have nowhere I belonged, but I also faced the danger of being discovered. Witches were the enemy. It was not unlike the Salem witch trials so long ago. If you had magic, you were instantly cast under suspicion and despised.

I'm called a dark witch today. A bad, evil witch. But what choice did I have? I had to either deny my birthright of using magic and live as a mundane human, or I had to find a source of protection—which meant being willing to do whatever spells our benefactor might request.

And before you interrupt, yes, I know how miserably ironic it is to say that I didn't want to be denied my birthright of practicing magic, yet I became the go-to witch for placing suppression curses on unborn children.

I didn't come up with the idea. My client did. This was someone I couldn't deny because they were part of my protectors. My "friends" who made sure I wasn't persecuted for being a witch like so many others were. Being someone's tool was the only way to stay safe.

And my powerful friends always wanted big favors. And they were always ready with an equal sacrifice for every request. They were the types who had plenty of people they wanted dead.

It was fine by me. I didn't know the people. I didn't personally go and stab them. I just had them bring me an article of that person, which allowed me to drain their life essence. Then, I made them a potion to do what they needed.

When I was asked the first time to suppress a fetus's shifter side, I wasn't sure I could do it. I hadn't messed with shifter magic yet. But my friends wouldn't be denied. They wanted it done in utero because any child already born would have already been identified as a shifter or not.

I had no idea what I was doing. I knew no other witch who practiced this kind of magic. We didn't have the internet to do searches, so all I had were my tomes, none of which contained any recipes for what was being asked of me.

So I studied. Combined spells. Made up my own and finally made a potion that I felt confident would work.

And just in time. They had the mother drink it—probably mixed in with juice or something—just a week before she went into labor, and I had to hope for the best. I wouldn't know if it worked until the child was born.

The day came, and the newborn infant had no shifter scent. It was a victory.

At least in my benefactor's eyes.

But I knew better. There was no guarantee on how this potion would work or for how long.

But that didn't stop new requests from coming in. Once the dark underground of the paranormal world learned what I could do, I became notorious—not just for shifters, but for other paranormals as well. My protectors enjoyed it—seeing as they took a cut of every payment. And I could charge heavily since I was the only one who was doing such a thing.

Not many other witches were willing to mess with children.

But why was I? Because I had no choice. If I tried to refuse, I'd lose the protection I'd so carefully built.

That didn't mean I was okay with it. Especially when my potions were used against other witches: spells against my own kind. Disgusting.

But you know what I told myself? I told myself that these fetal witches would never have to make the hard choices I did. They wouldn't have to come into this world with powers just to have the world turn on them. They wouldn't have to become a dark witch like me, trading favors for protection.

At least, that's how I justified it.

I still was worried, though. I didn't know if the spells would hold. The truth would show at puberty. Would the children's animals push through, or would they stay suppressed?

I tracked them all, ensuring I was prepared for the outcome if my potions failed. My benefactors would turn on me if they did.

The first child went through puberty with no change. One after another, they reached maturity, and my spells held.

I didn't dare think that was all there was to it, though. I stayed afraid of the day when my magic wasn't strong enough to keep the animal or magic side asleep.

Finally, that day came.

"And I knew it was over," the witch in the rippling mirror finished. "I packed my things and left. Changed my name, changed everything. Closed down my shop—which actually was a great little place, beloved by the town and tourists, you know. I loved finding and selling antiques more than I loved selling spells, but by the time I realized that, it was too late. I couldn't get out of what I'd gotten myself into."

Jeanie stood there, stunned. She'd expected the witch to have been the villain in the story, but she wasn't. She was someone who'd been used, who'd had no choice in the matter. Who'd done what they needed to survive, and who'd justified their actions by telling herself that her victims would be better off after the potions.

"Why are you telling us all this so easily?" Jeanie asked.

"Why not?" the witch through the mirror replied. "You deserve to know what happened to you and why. I wouldn't deny you that."

"But you won't tell us who you are or where you are."

"No, because you have no reason to know," the witch said. "Offering you the story means you get everything you need, with no reason to find me. I'm telling you everything I know."

"Then, can you tell us why this happened now?" Bliss asked. "Why Jeanie's bear emerged after forty years, not at puberty?"

"I can't tell you that," the witch answered. "Not that I don't want to, just that I don't know. I told you these potions were experimental. It's magic, not science."

"Is this happening to the others?" Jeanie asked.

"I don't know."

"I thought you tracked them?" Jeanie gave an exasperated sigh, looking to Bliss and Glynis, who had unreadable expressions. Edda had left the doorway, presumably too afraid to be so near a witch's mirror.

"I tracked them while I lived in town. While I was making sure they held," the witch replied. "When the first one failed, I packed up everything, cleared out my shop, and left. I'd have to pay. The dangerous people I worked for would make sure of it."

"Do you know why that one failed?" Bliss stepped into the bathroom and took hold of Jeanie's hand, knowing she needed added strength through this conversation.

"Maybe I did it wrong. Maybe the scales were tipped."

"Meaning what?"

"Meaning the life force had only so much power to give the spell. Maybe the life only had that many years left. That's what I assumed."

"So my father only had forty years to live if you hadn't killed him." The accusatory tone in Jeanie's voice silenced the witch. Finally, Jeanie asked, "Are you still there?"

"I told you the story. I'm sorry I don't know more than that. I don't have reason to sit around while you castigate me. Now, if you'd be so kind as to leave my house and prop the doors back up, I'll have someone come by and fix them later."

"Why are you keeping this place if you've never come back?" There were so many more questions Jeanie could ask, but she had no chance.

"Goodbye, bear."

The rippling stopped, and the apartment was silent again.

12

———

THEY LEFT THE WITCH'S PLACE—EVEN PROPPING UP THE doors as she'd asked.

Jeanie didn't know what to think. She'd been furious with the witch, but now she wasn't so sure. It wasn't like the witch chose to do dark spells, at least if her story was to be believed. It seemed like she did it out of necessity, and try as she might, she couldn't fault someone for doing what they had to for survival.

Glynis and Edda stayed quiet most of the ride. Bliss kept to subjects that were light. Learning more about Jeanie in general.

They contacted Sandy, and all agreed to meet up at a restaurant halfway between Edda's house and Georgetown.

"We're treating this as a celebration," Bliss said when they arrived and found Sandy already seated at the table. "We went there, we learned some information, and we can be proud of what we've accomplished."

It had become late, and Bliss suggested that she'd drive Glynis home in the morning if the elder wanted to stay at the alpha's house.

Glynis surprised everyone by saying she'd stay the night at Edda's.

Once everyone else was gone, and only Glynis and Edda remained in Edda's living room, Glynis turned to the other woman. "You really don't know anything about who was dealing with this witch?"

"Of course, I don't," Edda said, fiddling with her knitting project. "You know what people think of me. What they thought of me then. Simple-minded Edda can't handle reading the newspaper, let alone being in on a big sleuth scheme to subdue a baby bear."

"You learned where her shop was, though," Glynis pointed out. "You really weren't curious to see what she looked like? You never went down there?"

"Of course not! Especially not after Jeanie's father *died*. Curious or not, I wasn't reckless. Besides, I only learned the location of her shop after she disappeared, and no one could find her."

"I'm surprised you never sought her out to make some kind of bargain."

"Like what?"

"Oh, I don't know. To make your husband alpha?" Glynis shrugged.

"What a stupid idea," Edda snapped. "My *husband* to be alpha would be all I could ask for. Not even the most powerful witch in the world could have made *me* alpha."

Glynis chuckled. "Edda, you say you want the power, but you're not an alpha type. The idea of you leading is ludicrous."

"Screw you, Glynis." Edda focused on her stitches, not bothering to look up.

After a bit of time, when the only sound was Edda's needles clacking, Glynis asked, "We really are different, you and I, aren't we?"

"We are, and we're not. We're a lot alike in what we wanted from this world, but you did your own thing, and I did what was expected and lived a miserable life because of it."

"Don't say that." Glynis reached across the couch and placed a hand on Edda's, stopping her knitting and prompting Edda to finally look at her. "Your kids love you, and you love them. You're not alone like I am."

"You don't have to be alone," Edda said. "Even though I'm only married into the Bearstins, it's still enough for them to allow you protection under the sleuth."

Glynis shook her head, pulling back from Edda. She settled onto the couch, resting her arms across her chest. "You know we have to track her down now."

Edda's eyes snapped to her with a dangerous fear, the kind that appeared when an animal was frozen but would fight if you kept moving forward. "No."

"Edda." Glynis sighed and rubbed her forehead. "It's been long enough."

"Our sister isn't the witch who did this!" Edda snapped. "You and I both know that. We would have smelled a trace of her on Jeanie when we met her. We both went there today to make sure our sister wasn't involved, and we confirmed it! There wasn't a trace of her to be found!"

"She might know who this witch is." Glynis dug around in her bag and revealed a single gold button. "I found this in a corner in the apartment. It should be enough for Prudence to be able to trace it back to its owner."

"And what does it matter?" Edda asked, returning to her knitting. "We learned all there is to know."

"We haven't seen her in over seventy years. Do you really want to die without reuniting?"

"So that's what this is about? Getting Prudence to trace this other witch is just an excuse to force her to speak to us again?"

Glynis was silent as she thought about the last time the three of them had been together. "After all this time, you'd think we'd be changed. Different people with different lives. Grown apart. Mere strangers. But that didn't happen. When I saw you today, it was like everything that happened in my life without you disappeared, and I was whole again. Somehow, even though you're a crabby old bat, you're still a part of me."

Edda grumbled, not used to words of affection from her eldest sister.

"Tell me you didn't feel the same."

"So what if I did? Yeah, it was good to see you. But if you feel that way, then why didn't you tell that young bear I was your sister? And why didn't you tell her the truth about why you know so much about magic?"

Glynis took a breath, sorting out the reason for herself, as she hadn't really thought about it. "I guess even after a hundred years, even after all these decades of change and progress, it still feels like we can't admit to anyone that our mother was a witch and our father was a bear."

"And back then, it was worse to be mated to a witch than to even a regular human," Edda added. "We got used to hiding our lineage. Hiding that our father had to leave his sleuth for marrying our mother."

"Do you think we would have been better off if our animals had been suppressed? We could have fit in better."

"And Prudence never would have done all of her dark deeds." Edda finally placed her knitting on her lap and looked back at Glynis. "I blamed her. All these years, I blamed her for her actions, but only now, after the witch explained why she did what she did, do I understand why Prudence did it. I thought she chose to be dark. That she could stop at any time..."

"But she didn't have that choice." Glynis finished. "Edda, the witch's story today made me feel the same. We were too hard on her. We pushed her away, farther into her dark magic. When that witch finished telling her tale, all I wanted to do was find Prudence. I have to. Even if she doesn't want to hear my apology—"

"She's dark, Glynis," Edda interrupted. "You're imagining a situation where she'll accept our apology and embrace us. But you're leaving out the *fact* that she's evil."

"I know she's evil, Eddie," Glynis said, using the old familiar name. "It doesn't matter how happy we'll be when we see her, we have to remember that our sister might not have cursed Jeanie, but she did other dark and *very bad things."*

"We should stay out of it. Just tell Bliss about Prudence and let her and Sandy figure out if they want to interview her for information on the other witch."

Glynis gave her a long look. "I still love our sister and still have loyalty to her. Maybe we will have to tell Bliss and Sandy, but I feel like I want to face her first before we sic the public on her when she might not know anything."

"Doubtful," Edda muttered. "Those witches made it their business to know who was working in what area, who did what spells. She knows."

"Yeah."

"We really waited too long to reunite," Edda said, looking like her sad, littlest-sister self again, the same way she had when she was going off to kindergarten for the first time. Despite the white hair and wrinkles, Glynis would always see her as that little kid.

"You should tell Jeanie that we're sisters. She'll want to know," Edda added. "She'll want to hear it from you before Bliss says something to that effect."

"I will," Glynis replied. "Just like we need to track down Prudence."

"We?" Edda asked, her eyes filling with fear once again.

"I said what I said."

Jeanie spoke to Oscar over the Bluetooth the whole way home, telling him what all they'd done.

He was slightly annoyed by the fact that his wife had been in danger. He wasn't there to protect her, but she assured him it didn't seem like they were in any *real* danger. Plus, she was pretty sure the other three bears had it all under control.

When she finally made it home, she found Oscar inside, reading a book on the couch. She plopped down next to him and cuddled in.

"Hey, good looking," Jeanie said, smiling. "Long time, no see."

"Hey, yourself." He really was still so handsome after all these years.

She tilted her head up, and he met her halfway, kissing her. Her brain fogged, the alluring scent of her husband and the lingering excitement from the day combining.

"So, you don't look upset about not finding the witch."

Jeanie shrugged. "I don't think there's any point to finding her. I think I got what I needed. My life has already changed enough. I have a new bear side and a whole new bear family to fit in. I think I need to focus on those two things and not on a literal witch hunt."

"Well, can't blame you there," Oscar said, putting his book away.

"Hey, Oscar?"

"Yeah?"

"Wanna shift and go for a run?"

"Whatcha working on, Barb?" Beau asked as he walked up and kissed her head. "I figured you'd have been on the bed passed out already, too tired to even put on your pj's."

"I was tempted." Sandy looked up from her book and smiled at him. Her husband knew her so well after all these years.

He looked over her shoulder. "Suppression spells? You picking up witchcraft as a hobby I didn't know about?"

"No," Sandy chuckled, swatting at Beau. He always knew how to make her laugh and lift her spirits, as he had since they were many decades younger. "The mystery of this witch wouldn't let my brain shut down for the night."

"I've filled my network in. They'll let us know if anyone has any information on this witch."

Sandy sighed. "I don't know if there's a point to finding this exact witch or not. What I'm worried about is the people who have hidden powers. If we find the witch, could we get her to reverse the spells? Could we find the people and help them before the spell wears off? I keep thinking, what if there are pack members of ours out there? As their leader, we'd want them to know."

"I certainly agree with you there," Beau replied.

"It's unthinkable." Sandy sighed, turning back to the book. "There's gotta be some information, somewhere, that will help us find this witch... and find the people she cursed..."

Beau leaned past her, putting the bookmark on the page and closing the tome. "This mystery is bigger than this one book. It's going to take some time. Get some sleep, and we'll come back to it tomorrow."

Sandy reluctantly rose from her chair and accepted Beau's outstretched arm. He wrapped it around her, and she wrapped hers around him. Together, they went off to bed, the Georgetown pack leaders, always together, always ready to help their pack, come what may.

The End (For Now!)

How many midlife women are about to find themselves with some magic or supernatural abilities? Where will Sandy's search lead her? And what will happen when Glynis and Edda find their sister? Find out in future Midlife Unleashed stories!

If you'd like to read Ruby's story about finding her nieces—and falling for Paul!—check out The Better Part of Valor *by Mandy Rosko!*

ABOUT THE AUTHOR

Renee Hewett writes paranormal romance. Before becoming a full-time writer she worked in marketing, web writing, and editing. She's volunteered for at many events, such as C4 Comic Con, Can-Con, and Romancing the Capital.

ReneeHewett.com
Facebook reader group
Sign up for Renee's Newsletter

ALSO BY RENEE HEWETT

Furry United Coalition Newbie Academy

Goose and the Ocelot

Moose and the Narwhal

Zeus and the Raptor

The Nightshade Guild

Sunny Mage

Magic Clouded

Illuminating Time

Crimson Moon Hideaway

Chimera's Edge

Harpy's Escape

Flame and Mist